The Carol of the Reactors

Vishal Suchak

THE CAROL OF THE REACTORS

First published in India 2019 by Leadstart Publishing
Second edition published by Shriniketan Press

ISBN 978-93-5407-033-4

earthlingtrilogy.com

Vishal Suchak asserts the moral right to be identified as the author of
this work.

This book is a work of fiction and any resemblance to actual persons,
living or dead, events and locales is purely coincidental.

Contents

About the Author

Vishal turned towards writing after
a successful career in advertising and
digital communication, spanning across
Mumbai, New York and Jakarta.
A questioning mind and the need to share
his existential crisis with the world
have manifested in The Earthling Trilogy,
the first of which is The Carol of the Reactors.

Acknowledgements

With utmost thanks to my God-Mother, who I dare not presume to name. Who read my manuscript from cover to cover and offered support when I needed it the most.

To David who always gave me a leg-up with a smile. Especially when we were pitching to a stem-cells client. To Anton for breaking graphic novels down for me and revealing archetypes in a post-post-modern context.

To Joy, who smiles down at us from a higher abode, for helping me see the 'Orange-filter-sky' as an eternal magic-hour.

Professor Rohit Goel from Jnanapravaha for his insights into the criticism of Christianity by the followers of the 'One True God' and what it takes to be Kantian.

Being a professional agnostic from Advertising & Mass Communication, speaking of a "Kingdom of Heaven" in the context of being Kantian is bipolar, no? While I'm on the subject, I'd like to thank my psychiatrists Dr Krishna Aiyyar, Dr Karthik Rao, and Amrita Clements, mental health professional.

In this age of social media and collaboration, I have been blessed with many guides, masters, builders and collaborators in this process including but not limited to The Mother, my harshest critic and inner-voice.

Sincere gratitude is also owed to the editor, executive editor & publisher who made seminal contributions, augmented this book and made it possible respectively. And the second editor who swooped in at the last moment to save the day. Not to mention the various others who stumbled their way through my poorly structured and badly written stream of consciousness.

A special word of thanks is also due to Larasati who served with me as a brother-in-arms on the Avian Flu awareness campaign for the UN during my time at OgilvyOne, Indonesia.

Being drawn to the Abrahamic faiths, honestly speaking – faiths of all kind, I must admit that I chose the Church of the Seventh Day Adventists because it allowed me to speculate over an alternate reality in an earnest attempt to weave a tapestry of fact and fiction set in a parallel near future.

With nothing but love for all the children in the world. Counting myself as one, dear reader, please don't stop here. Do grant this attempt your consideration.

#HashedWhispers

Sometimes, the one who got away and the one who never left are one and the same, she muses, one hand on her belly as she reclines on the hospital bed.

Her entrance into the quarantine zone had been a bit of an event, and the Chief Councilman had come to the walls of the terrarium to receive her himself. "I could get used to this royal treatment," she had joked. But the official, taking her at face value, remained deferential.

Housed in a refurbished suite and given an all-access pass, she walked through corridors lined with the ailing and the infirm between her regularly scheduled check-ups. Her presence was acknowledged by one and all, with some even asking to be blessed as they knelt before her. The staff referred to her as The Mother.

Staring out of the windows at what she can see of the quarantine zone, her thoughts drift to the name she has chosen for her child, in memory of the one who slowly and unknowingly warmed her heart.

Just then, there's a knock on the door. After a brief pause Dr Hudson, holding the door ajar asks, "Mother?"

Hastily wiping the solitary tear making its way down her cheek, she rises to greet him. "Sir, do you need more samples? Any more tests to be done?"

"No," The good doctor replies simply, settling down on the only chair in the room.

"It's nice to see you like this," she says, seeing the scientist at ease and without the usual entourage of doctors and technicians. "I have great news," he begins. "But first, I'd like to know how you're doing. You haven't been feeling stifled, stuck in here, have you?"

"I'm quite comfortable actually," she replies, a little puzzled by this tidal shift in Dr Hudson's attitude.

"The Gospel truth, then. Based on the various progressive tests we've made from the amniotic fluid samples and the tests we've carried out on those who volunteered, you've made believers out of us all." Catching his breath to check his excitement he continues, "We've determined that it's not just the stem cells your child has been transmitting through the umbilical cord, but the very DNA itself that holds the key to a final solution."

"Really? For all mankind?" Her decision vindicated, a relieved smile spreads across her face.

"Yes," the good doctor replies. "We'll be able to engineer an antidote that we ourselves should be able to manufacture right from here. Hopefully we will be able to formulate a stable inoculation as well. I can't say for sure just yet, but in all probability it will be so. Or as the Pastor prefers to say, *may it be.*"

"Now, there is something else I wish to share," the doctor adds, his smile waning just a little. "But you must make a covenant to keep all of it in the strictest confidence."

"Yes, Dr Hudson, of course I do," The Mother replies.

Taking a deep breath, the doctor bares his soul. "Mine has been an influential voice in the resistance, and..." he adds, "I suppose, you know the rest..."

"What?!" she mouths the word inwardly, her lips pursed as she steadies her pulse. The way she has been taught.

"All we wanted was to negotiate," the doctor continues, his

voice laced with fervour. "If we had some sort of leverage, we thought, we could have accomplished something." But sensing the revulsion, Dr Hudson softens his voice. "We only wanted to put the proverbial gun to the head. We never took Josh for such a..."

103 DAYS AGO

1

Enter, The All-loving Hero

He moves through the decontamination chambers in automatic mode as technicians in bio-hazard suits run test after test, sending him from one section to another.

By the time he gets on the conveyor belt of the chemical scrub and wash process, the last of the lot, he starts to prepare himself for the role he will soon be playing. No matter how much time you spend counselling pre-teens, there is still no way of knowing what question will pop up when, and more importantly, how the answer will be received. And today being day one, the day of first exposure, the reactions are bound to be the most intense.

The cool breeze from the blowers on his privates, ticklish as always, jerks him back to the moment.

He has always been a little self-conscious and knows he has precisely fifteen seconds before the conveyor belt brings him into viewing range of the last supervising technician of the decontamination chambers—the first untainted human he'll be seeing without a gas mask on, the first human he'll make eye contact with. It's hard for him to tell whether his self-consciousness stems from his nudity or mutation.

Mutation - the side effect of an experimental antigen meant to protect him from the mutation itself. While the antigen succeeded in keeping him alive, the outcome turned out to be bizarre. His skin had taken on a radioactive green hue. His bone structure had remained intact as had his muscles which had become more pronounced and far stronger than they could have otherwise been. There were furry clumps of green hair on his shoulders, back, thighs and calves. And his eyes had become cat-like, luminous, like an orange-filter-sky when he narrowed them. The mutation had occurred gradually, ending abruptly once he had rapidly attained maturity. Just as it had for so many others who had ventured out into the quarantine zone inoculated with the more developed yet still insufficiently tested batches of the drug and survived. And even for those who had received the successfully tested samples but had stayed out far too long. Originally untainted, those survivors were arrested in various stages of mutation in these very same decontamination chambers on their way in, and were fated to stay out in the quarantine zone forever.

The mutation, being unique to each individual's genetic predisposition, varied from person to person. But the supervising technicians had seen it all and since Josh passed through on all work-days, six days a week, there was nothing left to see.

He dresses up quickly in the regulation gabardine overalls. Dabbing some of that lightly scented disinfectant on his chin and glad to be making the most of the facilities, he wonders who the survivors really are. Those within, or without?

Going back to days when he was stuck out there in the quarantine zone, from when he'd consider himself lucky to have a bath once a week, he nods at the peacekeeper standing guard with a half-smile and quickly steps inside the terrarium.

Filling his lungs with the clean air, he makes his way to the terminal to take the monorail from the entrance of the terrarium to Tower One. Knowing that blending in with the commuting human survivors is out of the question, he settles down on one of the seats, his head bowed low as if he were hunched over a device and starts prepping himself.

Picking up the pace as soon as he is out of the monorail terminal, he strides towards Room 255 of the counselling section. Or as everyone calls it, Tweenland.

His co-counsellor doesn't like it when he is late. And delights in his punctuality.

Chicks! Untainted human or mutated survivor, they're playing you all the time.

Taking the stairs on the double, he sees her soon enough.

Pretty.

Human.

Smiling.

Pearly teeth embedded in soft features sparkle through her amber skin. Almond shaped eyes twinkling, head erect with jet black hair framed by streaks of white. Amazon incarnate, she stands tall and proud, with an athletic build that can be hard to resist.

Seeing her alone in the room, Josh, in the most even voice he can manage says, "Hey Kilia, ready for today?"

2

Welcome to Tweenland

The tweens, all thirty of them, have been led to, and seated in, the darkened room which is quiet but for the whirring of the computer's hard drive. Josh knows the worst will come with the lights.

Kilia, hoping it is not before, launches the slide-show with a click and the screen fills up with a picture of an innocuous industrial complex. Even the ominous bio-hazard warnings do little to dampen the picturesque balance of science and humanity.

"This is the San Onofre Nuclear Power Generation plant," she begins, her voice controlled, sombre and personable. "Both its reactors were shut down in January 2012."

Click! Another industrial complex. This one even more subdued. Almost residential. "But this one, the Diablo Canyon Power Plant, was one of many nuclear facilities built near fault lines and still operational when the Pacific Ring of Fire lit up."

Click! A world map. Unlike with most maps, the focus is not a continent but on the Pacific Ocean. It features heat mapping, indicating the volatility of seismic activity across geographies. Her voice, still neutral but engaging just the same, continues, "This is the Pacific Ring of Fire, where volcanoes and earthquakes are formed. The ring, 40,000 km long, has 452 volcanoes and it's on this ring that 90% of all earthquakes and

15% of the world's largest earthquakes occur. All but three of the world's 25 largest eruptions from the last 11,700 years occurred at volcanoes on this ring."

Click! The map now features a multitude of red and yellow dots littered all about, superimposed on the previously displayed heat mapping of the seismic activity. A picture that speaks more than the thousand words to come. "There were 74 operational nuclear facilities running and 486 non-operational facilities with toxic waste. Plus surplus fissionable material spread across the ring when the apocalypse took place."

Click! The classic mushroom cloud of a nuclear explosion. "Unlike the two peculiarly named nuclear bombs—'Fat man' and 'Little boy'—that were set to explode before hitting the ground in Japan during the second world war, these explosions and leaks were all on the surface level. And so they were far more devastating."

Click! The ravaged remains of what once was the Diablo Valley. "This is what this site was like back then. Since the impact of land based nuclear contamination from just one nuclear facility was equal to 50 'Little boys', the holocaust was utter and complete."

Click! A world map featuring swathes of colour indicating nuclear fallout. A quarter of the planet has been blotted out and Africa is the only continent that remains entirely unaffected. "Most scholars agree that early humans first stood tall in Africa and migrated to populate our world. In a sense, Africa is doing it again."

Click! A chart outlining mankind's fate over a time-line. "By June 2013, six months after day zero, 11% of the world population was gone, 17% had terminal mutative disorders, 30% had non-life-threatening mutation—leaving less than half of humanity unaffected."

The lights come on abruptly while the pre-teens are still taking in all that has been said so far. Stepping forward ever so slightly, she says, "I am one of those unaffected. An untainted survivor."

"And I, like some of you, am a mutated human," Josh adds, without skipping a beat, but not stepping an inch out of his corner.

The lights stay on just long enough for the children to see each other and the counsellors, whose voices they have been hearing in the dark all this while, for the first time. Before anyone can react, Josh dims the lights gradually and the show goes on.

Click! A child's smiling face fills the screen. "This is Shanice." It's Josh doing the talking now. And he knows it is important for him to not only take things forward, but to do it just as well as she did. "Like some of you, Shanice is an untainted human survivor. Her mother is one as well."

Click! A picture of Shanice and her mother visiting her father in the quarantine zone follows. Smiles and hope on the faces of the united family notwithstanding, the bleakness of the visual is overpowering. "But Shanice's father, being a relief volunteer, got inoculated with an early batch of a radiation protection agent and ended up getting irreversibly affected by the fallout."

One of the children breaks down and starts to sob loudly. By this time, someone usually does. It is Kilia's job to console the tweens while Josh goes on with the show. "This is the quarantine zone," he continues, pointing out sections across the screen, "where Shanice's father lives with the rest of us mutated humans while Shanice and her mother live inside this domed terrarium with all the untainted human survivors. We are in the counselling section located in Tower One. This is Room 255. This, is Tweenland." After just the right amount of time, Kilia adds, "There are many such terrariums built along regions worst affected by the earthquakes and the consequent nuclear fallout."

Click! A picture taken from a helicopter of the domed terrarium as it was being built years ago fills the screen. And Josh resumes, as per the script, "Our terrarium, Eden (925), the one we're all in right now, was built before you were born. Once the honey-comb dome was set in place and irradiated, untainted survivors who volunteered with the United Nations were able to live within and venture out into the quarantine zone for relief work."

Click! A recent picture of the Diablo Terrarium with the quarantine zone around it and the outlying farmlands. "This is how our self-sufficient and integrated society now lives, in and around Eden (925)."

"Within the dome or outside in the quarantine zone, mutated or otherwise, we are all human." Having rushed his way through his part he gets to the last bit, the only assurance he finds solace in, "As long as we choose to remain that way."

He then turns the lights back on gradually and retreating into a corner, braces himself with a half-smile.

Kilia, having busied herself handing out paper napkins and comforting the tweens in the dark, steps into the centre of the room.

"I can see that some of you are troubled, now, and many might wonder why your parents never told you about any of this before," she says as soothingly as she can, her Lacanian training taking over. "I'm sure there are, and there will be, many questions. We are here to answer them all, but for now I want all of you to get to know each other. And so, dear Children of Diablo, get your chairs in a circle around me and settle down. We're going to introduce ourselves one by one."

#DeckOfTropes

#LoveUnspoken

Josh of Diablo	Child Counsellor, Construction Worker	#AllLovingHero #PostApocalypticDog #FineBalance
Kilia Bagyoko	Child Counsellor, Masters in Psychology from Columbia University	#EmpathicHealer #DaddysGirl #AcingBechdel

#LoveConsummated

William Yuen	Administrative Associate, Chief Administrator's mentee	#EpicFail2012 #IgnoredExpert #DeviceSetToScramble
Paige Turner	Personal Assistant to the Chief Administrator, Eden (925)	#SnarkBait #AuthorSurrogate #PinkCollarJob

#UntaintedSurvivors

Chief Administrator, Eden (925) The U.N. mission at Diablo Valley, California		#ReasonableAuthority-Figure #FreudianExcuse
Jorge, No. 2.	Deputy Chief Administrator for Eden (925)	#TheOnlyBeliever #UndyingLoyalty
Alasco Bagyoko	Kilia's Father, Tribal Warrior, Factory Worker	#ImmigrantParent
Khady Bagyoko	Kilia's Mother, Home Maker, Nanny	#ImmigrantPatriotism

#MutatedHumans

Dr Alfred J Hudson	Former Biogenetic Research Scholar	#AchillesInHisTent #BrokenPedestal
David Cohen	Former Documentary Film-maker, Councillor for the Mutant Outreach Program	#JazzAficionado #TheScribe #TrueAgnostic
Viktor	Former Street Artist, Precious Metal Harvester	#NotInThisForYour-Revolution #CulturedBadass
Aiko-chan	Viktor's Pet Peeve	#OneSceneWonder #EnsembleDarkHorse
Pastor Felipe	Pastor for the Seventh Day Adventist Church in Diablo Valley	#TheProphet #DeusExNukina

#CuteKids

Tidjane Bagyoko	Kilia's brother, once removed. Man-U-Supporter	#SecondGeneration-Immigrant #RedArmy
Poo	Single-Parent Child	#FreeRangeChild
Junior	Mr & Mrs Cooper's last hope	#RedState #ArmedWithFaith #NotCannonFodder
The Rapping Tween	Trailer Park Rabbit	#BoxcarChild

STILL, A 103 DAYS AGO

3

Green tea & Geopolitics

The Chief Administrator is at it again. Doing his patented soulful, understaffed, overworked, servant-of-the-people routine. An act that he has put on for so long, and with such consistency, that even his staunchest critics in the administration have been won over. That, and the fact that he is remarkably good at his job.

It stands, however, in stark contrast to the manner in which he conducts his orchestra with his pen.

A pensive look on his face, the tips of his lips curved appropriately, he takes in the last of the weekly reports from his Chiefs-of-Staff. "Food rations have been replenished."

Click.

He clicks his pen thrice after taking in each piece of information.

Click.

Expressing his satisfaction.

Click.

And queuing up the next section head.

"Our water supply is a little low but that's to be expected."

"Any problems at the waterworks?" the Chief Administrator asks, his thumb frozen above the clicker, as he turns to face the Chief of Engineering.

"No sir, just a minor shortfall of raw water due to the recent contamination."

Barely have the words left the Chief of Engineering's mouth that William, the Administrative Associate – a future Chief Administrator in grooming, interjects. "Do we need to impose any cutbacks?" he asks, darting a quick glance at the head of the table out of deference and continues, "Protocols for the preservation of essential commodities and everything," cocking his head back at the Chief of Engineering.

"Let's hold out as long as we prudently can, young William," the Chief Administrator benevolently cuts the tension the young ivy-leaguer has built so far with his repeated second guessing of the Chiefs-of-staff. "We don't wish to alarm the citizens."

Click, click, click.

"Alors, the situation with the science division is more or less the same," the thickly accented Chief of Science reports, implying the failure of the latest batch of vaccines. "But the production of the antidote is on at full *capacité*," the handsome Frenchwoman, a biogenetic research scholar from the University of Lyons, masks her frustration behind a deceptively ditzy exterior.

Originally brought in to oversee the manufacture of antidote, the Chief Administrator had quickly expanded Dr DeChampeaux's role, requisitioned equipment and even allocated additional resources.

Click, click, click.

He had neither an understanding of the underlying science nor any reason to believe her efforts at finding a cure would meet with success but he allowed it for brownie points.

"And the peacekeepers, Captain, are they enjoying their

supplemental exercises and manoeuvres?" He asks, turning to face his Chief of Security.

The former Navy SEAL, hardened by his training and scarred by tours of duty in the Middle East, was without a doubt the toughest man in the room, possibly even the terrarium itself. But he reddens as he answers, "Any complaints, sir?"

"No, nothing out of the ordinary," the Chief Administrator replies airily, taking pleasure in making this specimen of manhood squirm. "That you are making men out of... them, is appreciated, both here and at the H.Q."

"I'd like to thank you all for your continued service to humanity," the Chief Administrator concludes, rising slowly, "and I wish you a good day."

"If you could all, like, follow me to the pantry," lighting up as she says this, Paige, the Chief Administrator's personal assistant comes into her element. She has done nothing so far beyond recording the minutes of the meet on her iPad. "There's an assortment of beverages including orange juice and green tea," she adds.

Noting William's eyes trailing Paige as she leads his Chiefs-of-Staff out of the conference room with mild amusement, the Chief Administrator turns to his deputy. "Before I forget, No. 2, when's your next scheduled evaluation of the quarantine zone?" His disdain for mutated humans is well-cloaked and in line with the office he occupies. But before his deputy can reply, he adds, "Miss Paige would like to accompany you."

The Deputy Chief Administrator looks up briefly from his iPad, a quizzical look on his face but saying nothing, pulls up his scheduler. "I'm going back on the 27th of this month, Chief."

"Very good. Let her know, won't you? And William, you should make a sortie too. When would you like to go?"

"I've just arrived, sir," William answers with a poker face. "And as soon as I'm done with surveying the terrarium, I'll be glad to step outside. Thank you for asking."

"Right. No. 2," the Chief Administrator, turning back to his deputy, adds, "Could you check in on our Head Auditor? Apparently, he's come down with something. Not that I mind his deputy delivering the weekly report on his behalf, but I'd like him to know that his presence is missed by us."

"*Si*, Chief, I'll do that as soon as we finish."

"So William, what did you think of today's meeting?" the Chief Administrator persists.

"It was good, sir," William replies, choosing his words carefully. "On agenda, succinct yet comprehensive," he says, parroting the text-book definition of the prescribed ideal.

Click.

"Given that this was the first time I met with some of the division heads," William adds hastily, "And being unfamiliar with some of the projects..."

Click.

Realizing he's two strikes down, William pauses, takes a deep breath and starts afresh. "What sort of training does the Chief of Security put the peacekeepers through? And does it result in complaints of a volume large and sustained enough for there to actually be an acceptable level?"

The Chief administrator turns to his Deputy with a smile.

"These are tough times, you see," No. 2 begins explaining in his good-natured way. "Times the Captain has trained his whole life for. And that too at an inhuman level. Some of our peacekeepers, like many young volunteers, take up postings more as a way of seeing the new world rather than offering service. Tough situation, tough times... and when you put a tough man in the mix... It started when a few of the peacekeepers, fresh off the boat, you see, began applying for transfers within days of their arrival. But it's all good now."

"Thank you, No. 2. I'll wait to hear about your social call at the Head Auditor's," the Chief Administrator dismisses his deputy who nods respectfully and leaves.

"Did Paige mention green tea, Chief Administrator?"

Getting yet another amused nod, William excuses himself for a taste of home.

Left to himself, the Chief Administrator leans back in his chair. Swivelling, letting his gaze sweep across all he sees through the wall-sized windows in the conference room of the administrative office, up in the highest part of the dome. Delicately perched on a needle like elevator shaft. Like an all-seeing eye. And he thanks his stars yet again. Or the gods. Or whatever powers that be, the ones that landed him this position within the Diablo Terrarium. He himself had been the most surprised when the delegates from the United Nations had made the announcement, laying emphasis on all he brought to the table. Especially the fact that a person in his prior position was bound to be most open to and accepting of all deviations and uniqueness. Not everyone was happy with the decision but no one ever argued with the United Nation's delegates. Not a single member of the Mutant Council, not even he himself, the now reigning Chief Administrator.

"Thank you for the tea, sir," William says upon his return, a satiated look on his face.

"Bú kèqì xiándì," the able administrator replies in a flawless accent.

"I didn't know you spoke Mandarin, sir..."

"Yes. But just a little." The Chief Administrator pockets his pen with grace and resumes, "So, it's almost been a week since you've arrived. And I haven't really been able to give you any face time. Let's redress that over a walk, shall we?"

On their way out, the Chief Administrator pauses, "Miss Paige, I'm stepping out for a bit. Hold the fort, won't you?"

"Yes, sir," she gushes, "I totes will."

Politely stepping aside to let her pass, the Chief Administrator strides through the office with William in tow and proceeds to the doorway. As they step through, both the peacekeepers standing guard outside snap to attention and salute him. One of them resumes his post while the other, Jan, follows them to the elevator.

As they descend through the lower and more populated levels of the offices, he nods several times as his presence is acknowledged by all who join them in the elevator. But he maintains a stoic silence having made it a habit never to speak to anyone during his rounds. That was left to No. 2.

It is only when they are in one of the emptier walking tracks of the garden built in the circular area between the twelve towers, with Jan following at a respectful distance, that the Chief Administrator opens bluntly, "Why, pray, are you here William? Because you're not here for the sights, that much I can tell."

William, won over by the Chief Administrator's hospitality and his no-nonsense treatment of matters at hand, opens up as one would to a true mentor. "Honestly sir, coming from a family of influence, I could have easily obtained a posting at one of the terrariums on the coast of China. In fact, back when I was applying to graduate schools, my father had my personal-mission essay ghost-written for me. I did need the help then. But now, I wish to make it on my own steam."

"Admirable. Go on."

"And one can't do that without stepping out of cocoons," William continues, "or in my case, literally stepping over protective walls."

"And do you like what you have seen so far?"

William, almost as if he were waiting to be asked this, responds emphatically, "I don't have access to the privileged reports you receive, sir, but as far as I can tell, humanity has never been more at peace and at work in harmony. The survival of the species seems to have transcended the self-interest of individuals, communities, regions, even nations. And I find that very satisfying."

The Chief Administrator's smile remains fixed but the cynicism in his eyes isn't lost on William. His smile vanishes. His eyes narrow into slits.

"One such as you," the Chief Administrator illuminates, "would surely know of the Bilderberg Group."

"Yes sir, of course. Conspiracy theorists have cried themselves hoarse." William mutters audibly, his head bowed. "Beyond a point, the Bilderbergers didn't even bother denying but began trying to project themselves in good light."

"Yes, well..." the Chief Administrator casts a glance over his shoulder to see if Jan is still following and continues, "their might is still intact, their tentacles deeply embedded in high places, if you catch my drift. And while we're on the subject, the much-maligned mighty military-industrial complex of yesteryears has reinvented and insinuated itself within the biogenetics sector as well."

"Oh?!" William exclaims, his eyes open but gazing into the middle distance. "So the new war is against extinction?"

"Precisely!" the Chief Administrator resumes jovially. "Like the space race, drugs, terror—it's now all about patenting the Final Solution. Whether it be an inoculation with permanence, or better yet, a cure that reverses mutation. And then there's our dependence on fossil fuels which is at an all-time high since we dare not go nuclear."

"Of course..." William surmises, "The equilibrium always reasserts itself."

"Suffer no delusions, young William, there is always an agenda." Not wanting to disillusion his protégé any further, the Chief Administrator eases up, "But there's the silver lining as well. Equilibrium, as you called it. And I'm not referring to the Middle Eastern hardliners and their delirious reactions to the obliteration of Hollywood and Japan, Sodom and Gomorrah according to them. They would've probably burned through all their Arab-money in celebration had they not realized that the fallout would reach their part of the world someday. Now they outsource terrarium construction projects to what's left of the first world, of course. But I speak of our untainted re-settlers, most of them from Africa. Airlifted and brought here at great expense to populate this terrarium and others like it. After centuries of suffering, seeing them amongst the privileged is... Well, irony for one is poetic justice to another."

Awed by the geopolitical ramifications, William lets an unfiltered thought through, "And to think, those who were once brought here as slaves are now the masters."

"Ha!" the Chief Administrator exclaims. "I wouldn't go that far. We are volunteers, xiándì, not slavers. And when it comes to our role in particular—to all the untainted human survivors within the confines of this dome, the mutants out there as well—we, the Administrators, are figureheads. Father figures at best. My deputy and I, we make a good team, and I welcome you to find your place in our configuration."

At sea but not wishing to lose face again, William walks in silence.

After a few moments, the Chief Administrator resumes, "What I want you to understand today is that we all suffer from, and I say this at the risk of sounding flippant, daddy issues."

As a smile slowly begins to dawn on William's face, the Chief Administrator continues, "In these times when god-addicts question their cherished beliefs, our biological fathers are all we're left with. In some cases, our admirable and loving fathers are no more. In others, they were neglectful to begin with, so one way or another, there's that gap. Or, in your management speak, the sweet spot."

"Why don't you shadow No. 2 today, William," the Chief Administrator instructs as they're stepping back into the Administrative Office, "and give me a report first thing tomorrow morning."

Seeing his Associate look longingly at the pretty young thing outside his office beyond the glass walls in the distance, he leaves William with a parting thought. "Daddy issues, xiándì, everyone with a daddy has issues."

So I got an email from Tammy today... Not that I don't appreciate all she did for Caleb and me, but she really gots to get some of that bitterness out of her system, or get laid! xD

And I get it, mum died when we were young, pops went into a beer-soaked coma in front of the TV. Guess she can't deal with me doing so well without her. And now Caleb's signed on for peacekeeper training as well. Maybe she'll get it when pops' liver cirrhosis finally does him in.

The bitch still be tripping me with the 'You abandoned us' shit, but what else was I to do? There's only so much Long-Island-Pie you can stuff down your throat going thru 'the texting your ex Jason Mraz lyrics' phase before you realize you gotta move on gurl. Hate on me all you like. What I got, I paid for.

Big change though, from a trailer park in North Amityville to this place. I still remember my first day here. Big Chief set aside an hour just to orient me. And even that wasn't enough. *facepalm*.

The man is a freakin' machine!!! xD He's in the office from 7 to 7 everyday, taking one meeting after another. And he crams in squash, a swim, a 15 minute power-nap and transcendental meditation as well. Whatever that is.

Keeping up with him is cray, but guess I'm doing ok now. Taking dictation, transcribing his voice memos, bringing him tea, manning the desk—that's cake. What stresses me out is staying on top of his schedule. He has a to-do list that he runs in parallel and he changes it around at least twice a day. Sometimes I think he does it just to mess with me.

Yea right... I wish...

As he started off with me on Day One, I was like, Ze OR Hir, bitches!! That clear skin, the lean frame, but then I realized he was very polite. And British. Still doesn't rule out Ze & Hir though.

And of course he's British! That accent, the vocabulary... Taking down his first memo, I was like whoa, whoa, whoa... Thank the internet for autocorrect, or I'd spend half my time looking those

 #WorkSleepRepeat   **Follow** • • •

words up. And that guy at the UN, he must be super important considering how often Big Chief writes to him.

I guess he has to. So much backstabbing and shit going on below the surface here. But I mean c'mon, we're UN volunteers ffs! And the things I've overheard in the cafeteria. The meanest one was about how the clicky pen is, like, his pacifier. So what if he's a little high-handed? If only those tools got over themselves, looked through the hard smile and caught just a glimpse of the pain in his resting bitch face. Sheesh! I sound so lame; I'll stop here, cos I'm crushin on him hard enough as it is.

#TruthHurts #LoveHurts #FineLinesBetweenTruthAndHurt #FineBalance #CestLaFrance #CestLaVie #CestSiBon

Scan code to visit Paige's blog
and connect with her on facebook

4

We belong to the Administration

"Miss Paige, a cup of tea would be lovely," the Chief Administrator announces as he steps into his chambers, startling her. Clearly she hadn't expected him back so soon.

"And I need you to take down a memo for Rolfe, so do bring your clicker in as well."

Paige rushes to the pantry in the back of the Administrative Office and returns quickly with a cup of steaming hot water on a saucer. Stopping by her desk to get one of the green teabags the Chief Administrator had given her, part of his personal supplies, she drops it in the cup. Taking her iPad in hand for the dictation she'll be taking, she walks up to the door of the Chief Administrator's chambers, knocks and enters after a brief pause.

The Chief Administrator now stands with his back to the door as he gazes out of the windows. He turns around only when he hears the clink of the cup and saucer being placed on his table and starts off right away. "Dear Rolfe, it has been nearly a week since I last wrote to you. I will be submitting the bi-monthly report to all five of you supervising delegates for terrariums in North America as always but for now I wish to present a short and informal memo touching upon key points."

He dictates rapidly, knowing Miss Paige, whose fingers tap dance across the screen, would manage just fine. "Our precious metal harvesting teams are truly earning their credits. Yields of nucleo-synthesized gold are at an all-time high. Sadly, Dr DeChampeaux reports that they are not any closer to a final solution than they were before."

Taking a delicate sip, he continues, "It has been a while since I addressed the assembly of construction workers but I will be doing that soon enough. I'm also including a film that should give the resource allocation department at Geneva a better picture of the harsh ground realities we deal with. That reminds me," the Chief Administrator suddenly changes his tone, breaking away from the dictation, "has David come in yet? Wait, Miss Paige, don't write that down. I'm asking you if David has come in... Has he?"

"Councilman David, from the quarantine zone?" Paige asks vacantly. "Um, he must have come in after you did. I saw him in the waiting area as I was stepping in."

"Well, send him *in*," the Chief Administrator exhorts. "I've gone to some lengths to get him what he needed to finish the film, and I'm positively aching to see it."

"So, Councilman, are we ready for the world premiere?" the Chief Administrator asks, as soon as he is face to face with David.

Is he making a joke, David wonders, *or trying to be encouraging*. "I'd really like you to decide for yourself, Chief Administrator; it's been a while since I've done this. Amazed as I am that you managed to procure the equipment for us, I have to admit that the production value isn't quite what it should be. Please consider that."

Upon the Chief Administrator's bidding, Paige lowers the blinds on the windows and assists David with plugging the camera to the large screen on the wall facing the Chief Administrator's desk.

As David packs up the camera and the Chief Administrator opens the blinds a few minutes later, there's a knock on the door. "I'm sorry, Chief," the deputy chief says, peeping in. "I couldn't find Paige outside so I took a chance."

"That's fine, No. 2. Miss Paige must be in the restroom, trying to get a hold of herself. And as I was just about to tell David, the presentation he's made for us is quite moving. I'd love to hear what you think of it."

David half rises from his seat and nods respectfully at the Deputy Chief Administrator in acknowledgement.

"*Hola*, David. How're you doing? How are things in the quarantine zone?" No. 2 inquires.

"They're as good as they can be, No. 2. I'm sure you'll get to see it all on your next visit."

"*Si*, David, *si*," replies No. 2 with a smile. "But you have the broadest and deepest view so I ask."

"So David, great job," the Chief Administrator interjects, taking charge of the room once again. "Will you be leaving soon or do you have any other gifts for us?"

"Oh. No, Chief Administrator," David replies, "this is all for now. I'm glad you like it."

"Oh it's good alright, now to see if it will have its intended effect," the Chief Administrator concludes.

"I'll get going then," David says, taking the hint with dignity. "There are some visits to be made, errands to be run."

Barely has the door shut after David's somewhat awkward departure, that the Chief Administrator turns his full attention towards his deputy. "You don't like David much, do you, Jorge?"

Sensing the informality, No. 2 is frank, "His past political affiliations aside?"

"Sit, Jorge, sit."

Even as he takes a seat, No. 2 continues, "And David's been known to keep all sorts of company."

"But he heads the outreach program. It's his job to reach out and associate with all sections of the mutated human community."

"Well, then I don't know what to say, Chief..." No. 2 trails off.

"Alright, so you're not entirely comfortable with him."

Taking a moment to get his thoughts together, No. 2 draws in a long breath and speaks with a finality that he reserves for only those times when he is alone with his superior. "He is where he is because of a documentary he made about Native Americans in the area, you see, and here you have him making another about a larger and an even more hard-up group of people?"

"I see what you're saying, Jorge," the Chief Administrator soothes, knowing full well he can never risk alienating his Deputy. "But I'm sure you'll see him in a different light once you see the film he's shot for us. Besides, the film is for the eyes of the folks at H.Q. only. Other than the three of us, Paige included, no one else even knows the film exists. Now Jorge, I'd like both you and William to have a look. Do that in your office; David has uploaded it onto our systems but you will need to use your personal security authentication to access it since it's classified. Once you're done, have William put together a series of hard-hitting statistics—suicide rates, infant mortality, the percentage of mutants living on the streets—that sort of thing. The film is moving, of course, but it won't get us a pretty penny without some troubling numbers to back it up. And would you be so kind as to send Miss Paige in. Hopefully that child has finished powdering her nose, or whatever it is kids do these days. I have to finish my dictation."

A conspiracy theorist sits at his desk. Itching for his next fix. Unsure if he is asleep, awake, or both. *There is nothing new under the sun*, his father once bellowed. *Ever wonder why children always draw the same picture with the sun always at the top-right?*

But that's the eye of the truth looking at itself, sir, William had whimpered back.

You possess no control over yourself my son, the father remarked remorsefully, letting go of William's hair as he saw the tears well up in his son's eyes. *I see too much of myself in you*, his father had whispered as he let his son go.

I know, William had replied, under his breath.

Reminding himself that there is no such thing as authority, only control, William straightens his back and steps out of his cave of solitude to make his way to the office of the toughest man in the terrarium. Returning with a satiated look on his face, William begins reverse-ego-googling for the nth time to erase his digital footprints. A digital-forensic expert himself, he leaves no stone unturned. *In order to inflict the maximum damage upon the administration*, he hears his own voice, *one must occupy the optimal position within the administration.* His multiple devices, multiple IP addresses and his well-guarded perch on the Dark Web were all hidden by avatars of Mystique because of the rule of the interwebs: there are no girls online. And on the platform, everything is porn. The brutal colonization of his race by the so-called higher yellows, of the five colour flag, devours him. *The Wikipedia hypothesis for the Olympic flag colours is just as good,* he thinks. *Unstable isotopes are the only way for fission and fusion.* But reproduction engenders him powerless. His never-beginning-never-ending search for his Eve, his primordial Lucy, has taken him far and wide. *Sometimes that is just a beginning,* he thinks to himself, because everything is just a perspective and there is nothing he isn't willing to do for true love, even if it lies behind blue eyes. Even if it entails dropping a bomb on the Hadron Collider.

5

The Truth, The Whole Truth, And Nothing But The Truth

Back at Tweenland, the introductions have been made. The initial shock has taken a back seat and bewilderment has given way to curiosity.

Breaking the truth to the children at this point in their lives and in this manner—first a cold splash of devastating reality, followed by co-habitation within the terrarium for three months with time enough for acceptance—this methodology and the modules for the duration of the camp had been designed by a panel of leading child psychologists, educators and living legends recognized by the United Nations.

As this is still Day One, there are no structured activities but free form games where the children have greater control in who they interact with as Josh and Kilia supervise, providing encouragement and a steady supply of smiles. The sessions will steadily fall into a more regulated yet customized schema in the days to come as per the curriculum. One designed painstakingly to sensitize the tweens to the dire situation that humanity finds itself in, and to each other.

Building bonds within a small group at this impressionable age will lead to greater unity and harmony for one and all in the long run – the stated goal.

As is to be expected, the mutant kids gravitate towards Josh, instantly identifying him as one of their own while Kilia is the centre for the untainted human children. By the time the games end, most of the kids are sweating and there are laughs all around. It's time for the last part of the day - the pairing, and both Josh and Kilia share a smile of relief.

Kilia, being the untainted human and host counsellor, takes the lead. "Alright kids, soon it will be time to go home." And before the mutant tweens can react, she quickly adds, "Those of you who came in from the quarantine zone must have come in through the decontamination chambers, yes? Now I know that whole song and dance sucks, so for the duration of this camp, you'll be staying with the family of one of the untainted kids from this group itself, inside the terrarium."

"Unlike you lucky ones, I have to keep going through the decontamination chambers every day," Josh quickly says his bit with a wide smile on his face knowing that staying away from their own families for three months is bound to cause anxiety to the mutant kids.

"And once we're done with the camp," Kilia resumes, "all the untainted human kids will come out to the quarantine zone to drop you back to your homes."

"Will they stay with us for three months as well?" one of the mutant kids asks. "There's barely enough room for us in our tent, ma'am."

"No sweetie, the inoculation provides protection to untainted humans for twelve hours only," Kilia replies. "And please call me Kilia. There's nothing for you to worry about because we'll visit all the way up to your doorstep and say our goodbyes there and then. But you can write letters to each other and can always meet when you grow up and find work inside the terrarium."

Taking his cue, Josh adds, "Like how I work at this camp for pre-teens such as yourselves. So, it's in and out every working day for me."

"Can't you stay in here all the time with us?" one of the particularly adorable untainted children asks. She's only eight but at Tweenland ahead of schedule, because of her single mother's slipup with parental lock settings. "I can sleep with mommy," she cooes, "and you won't have to go through that decontamission chamber Kilia was talking about. I'll ask for permission when she comes. She never says no to me."

"That's against the rules given to us by the United Nations, Poo," Kilia replies. "And, we can't be unfair to all the other mutants who come in and leave day after day just because Josh is a bit of a big green teddy-bear, now can we?"

Josh breaks into an embarrassed grin as some of the mutant and most of the human tweens giggle. "So," Kilia resumes, "all fifteen of you mutant pre-teens are going to be spending three months with us and it's time to choose who stays over with whom."

As the Deputy Chief Administrator steps out of the Chief Administrator's chambers, he feels himself relaxing a little.

His brief discussion with the Chief Administrator about David aside, the weekly reports with the Chiefs-of-Staff had gone well, and the house call he had made at the Head Auditor's had gone just as smoothly. With William silently following him, No.2 begins humming one of his favourite tunes.

Knowing that the Chief Administrator preferred to keep his distance, especially from his subordinates even within the Administrative Office, No. 2 often went out of the way to lighten the mood in the otherwise taut environment.

"*Hola,* John," he greets one of the junior executives as he passes him by through the maze of cubicles. "How's the family doing?"

"They're doing just fine No. 2," comes the reply.

"Give your father my regards."

Continuing in the same friendly manner, chatting with everyone he comes within speaking distance of and smiling at everyone he makes eye contact with, No. 2 gradually makes his way out of the administrative office.

As he opens the door and sees a couple blocking the exit, arguing with the peacekeepers on security detail, his heart sinks a little. "Pardon me, I'll just squeeze through," he waits to be excused, hoping it isn't about the children.

"We'd like to see someone about this mutant kid we're supposed to room with us. They tell us it's standard procedure and all, but that don't make it fair to my family, now do it?" the man says gruffly, not budging an inch.

"I'm on my way to the counselling section where your child and the mutated human child you refer to will be waiting. Why don't we discuss this on the way there?" No. 2 graciously suggests.

Now the woman begins speaking, her voice even more agitated than her husband's, "No mister, we ain't going nowhere until we meet this high and mighty Chief Administrator of yours and get this mess cleared up. We know what he used to do in the old world and no fairy-lover decides who comes and goes out of my home, no matter how many party favours he arranged for some faggot UN official."

"Amen!" her husband adds.

Groaning inwardly, No. 2 begins with the short speech he must have made innumerable times before. "The past notwithstanding, he is the Chief Administrator appointed by the UN. His prior work experience in efficiently dealing with the exotic with an open-mind is precisely why he has been selected to run this facility. Do you have any idea about the size of that spa? And how well it was doing under his management? It became the largest hospitality franchise in Thailand, you see, so I suggest you show a little respect." His voice had perceptibly hardened and this wasn't lost on the couple. Even William finds himself impressed by this shift in disposition of the otherwise jolly Deputy Chief Administrator. "And allow me to remind you, this being a coveted post, there were no shortage of applicants either," No. 2 adds for good measure. "So why don't you calm down and let me help you instead?"

"And you are?" the man asks.

"I'm the Deputy Chief Administrator. Please call me No. 2. Everyone does. Now, as I was saying, let's talk on our way to the section where the children are waiting."

"You hold it right there, Mr No. 2," the man places his right hand roughly on No. 2's chest, stopping him dead in his tracks. "We've done a bang-up job with our petition so far and we sure as hell ain't going nowhere until we get this sorted out good and proper!"

The peacekeepers, their patience long exhausted, respond to the menacing tone and physical contact with swift and extreme prejudice, grabbing the man's hands and pinning him against the wall. "Mr Cooper, the official you just tried to shove is the second in command for this terrarium and there's no room for violence here, or anywhere," the guard who had been arguing with the man when No. 2 walked in on them, warns over the woman's scream. "I can only release you if your cooperation with all authority figures and compliance with all rules, codes and directives is assured. Nod if you understand what I just said."

The man, now cowed down, nods quickly. After getting an approving nod from No. 2 as well, the peacekeeper pulls the man back just a little and shoves him against the wall as he releases him.

"Mr and Mrs Cooper, is it? Come, let us put this unpleasantness behind us and get on the elevators," No. 2 resumes, back to being himself. "I'll explain everything to you on our way. Trust me. There's nothing you have to worry about, you see. You are not the first family that's going through this, and unfortunately," a sigh escapes as he enunciates, "You won't be the last."

On the quiet ride to ground level, William makes a mental note to look up the files on the Coopers. *They managed to make it all the way up to the top floor of the Administrative Office*, he thinks to himself. *They must be well connected.*

Josh rises and addresses the children now seated in assigned pairs—the host children telling their mutated guests all about their families and homes as they've been instructed to. "Alright kids, have a great evening. I'm leaving now but starting tomorrow, I'll be staying with you all through to the end."

"Say bye to Josh, kids," Kilia says with a bright smile.

"Bye bye Josh!" the children say all at once in varying tones and volumes.

"And kids," Kilia continues, "if you're done with sharing and learning about life inside the terrarium, you mutant kids can tell your untainted buddies about your families out in the quarantine zone. And all of you, don't worry about being stuck in your homes anymore. Now that you know all we have learned today, we'll be taking you on a tour of the entire terrarium. Alright?"

As some of the children clap, Poo gets up right away thinking the tour is about to begin but sits down sheepishly as a few others break into laughter.

On his way out, Josh walks straight into No. 2, William, and the Coopers. His appearance and determined demeanour all but cause Mrs Cooper to faint. Mr Cooper, sensing this, steadies her right away, casting a questioning glance at No. 2.

"Josh!" No. 2 exclaims. "Meet the Coopers. Their child is one of your counselees and as you can see, we've arrived a little early." Having calmed his erstwhile interlocutor sufficiently, No. 2 continues, "Mr Cooper, this is Josh, one of our counsellors. He doesn't usually meet the parents till the very end of the camp due to his exceptional appearance. But he's a hit with the kids you see, aren't you, Josh?"

"Yes, No. 2," Josh replies, unsure of what to do or say next.

Mr Cooper, having worked extensively in the quarantine zone and having seen the strangest of the strange, takes it upon himself to be the bigger man and extends his hand politely. "That's a fine grip you have there, young man."

As Josh smiles politely, William wordlessly catalogues yet another experience.

6

Men At Work

Hitching a ride on one of the many trucks that frequent the perimeter of the apartment complex at the centre of the terrarium, Josh is soon on his way to his second job. The population residing in the tower complex will someday relocate to the housing projects currently underway. And the tower complex itself will be repurposed into a business district as mankind—human and otherwise—makes a smooth, if somewhat protracted, comeback. *Too bad I won't be around to see it,* he thinks to himself on his bumpy, dusty journey to the ever-expanding periphery of the already built housing projects.

When he finally gets there, he finds his crew busy at work and their crew chief, the warm and somewhat garrulous Mr Sebastian, turning away from his supervision to greet him heartily as always. "Hello, Josh, how was camp boy-o? First day and all. That's the reason ya coming in early, aren't ya?"

"Yes, Mr Sebastian," Josh says with the first smile of the day he genuinely feels. "I'm sorry I forgot to tell you yesterday."

He'd been spotted by Mr Sebastian one day on the monorail, when he was still in counsellor training. The crew-chief just struck up a conversation mistaking him for a fellow construction worker and the connection between them had formed and developed from that moment on. Over time,

Mr Sebastian had taken Josh under his wing and the kindly Irishman's support was as valuable as the credits Josh received for working at this hard job.

"Still getting it on with that West African Water Nymph in Tweenland, eh laddie?"

"Come now, Mr Sebastian, quit teasing. I've already told you about 'the rules' from counsellor training." Josh replies, hoping he isn't blushing through his greens.

"I've seen Kilia, ya know, many times. I was assigned to her family when they moved here and I'm friends with her father. Good people, the Bagyokos. It took them some time to adapt to life in the United States, what's left of it anyway, but they're me hearties now..."

Seeing his boss getting warmed up, Josh interrupts with a laugh, "I know, Mr Sebastian, I know. Since I'm here a little early, I'd like to join the crew before the first shift ends. May I?"

"Alright, alright. Great seeing ya! Jump right in."

Josh makes his way to the temporary shanty at the back where the gear is stored and wears the overalls specially tailored to fit his unique frame and build, followed by the gloves, his tool belt and then secures his helmet as quickly as he can.

They'd been building templatized four-bedroom housing structures for a while now and today would be no different. Josh had observed the smoothly functioning crew digging a large hole to lay a concrete foundation while talking to Mr Sebastian, work they had begun only the previous day. Picking up an automatic excavator, he heads out and jumps into the pit. Making an effortless landing with the burden of the excavator still in hand, he selects a spot and begins drilling.

Always concerned about his crew members resenting him

for the rapport he shares with the crew-chief and the far less physical task of counselling pre-teens for the first half of the day, he always gives his construction job all he has. Soon he's bathed in sweat like the others and has fit into their work-rhythm as well.

Three quarters of an hour later, when Sebastian brings the first shift to an end, the crew gets to have a water break. Despite their job being deemed among the most essential, there wasn't a watering hole where they could bond after work, so these breaks tended to be a little awkward. And so Josh admired Mr Sebastian all the more for running things as well as he did.

As the crew clambers back into the pit, a van pulls up and two men step out. The one carrying a clipboard busies himself making notes right away. The other, the burlier one, calls Sebastian over.

"Stall the ball, men," Sebastian announces, returning after a brief talk with the Administrative Executives. "We have a safety inspector and someone from Human Resources who would like to have a word with each of ya, one by one." As the crew stops working, he adds with a smile, "Don't go spilling any beans now."

By the time the inspection and interviews come to an end, the sun is close to setting and Sebastian hits the switch that powers the lamps illuminating the site. Peering down the pit that is now lit well, Sebastian instructs the five men doing the digging to stop and rolls out the measuring tape, lowering it all the way in. "Just a wee bit more to go at this position lads," he says, "and then we move to the other side." The crew, quite exhausted by now, wordlessly resumes work. Josh keeps at it with his quiet determination, making up for time lost with the inspectors.

"That's enough now. Come on up, catch your breath and get

cleaned up," Mr Sebastian calls out as soon as their target for the day has been reached, a little after the work day officially ends. And soon enough he's busy shaking everyone's hands, thanking them for their labour and apologizing for keeping them after-hours even though it was the inspection that delayed them all. He squeezes Josh's hand a little harder, and his grateful smile sparkles with pride.

The untainted humans on the crew get on the van they share for their commute to and from the apartment complex, leaving the mutated humans to wait for their own bus. This bus, assigned to transport the mutated humans back from various construction sites to the decontamination zone, finally arrives and Josh hops on board with the others.

After the tense and emotional first day at Tweenland, the heavy construction work had turned out to be therapeutic for Josh and he sits silently, drifting in and out of snatches of conversation his fellow mutated humans have—from friendships formed over these daily rides back to the exit of the terrarium together.

7

Behold, the Quarantine Zone

Walking through the much shorter exit zone of the decontamination chambers, Josh remembers the days when the transition from the terrarium to the quarantine zone was too much to take, night after night.

Inside, the untainted humans lived in a surgically clean environment. Everything was standardized, regulated; all the way down to the forks and knives and even the gabardine outfits they wore—apart from whatever apparel they had brought with them. And there was uniformity in the living quarters as well. *Happy little busy bees. Making and breaking their own honey.*

Leaving the other homeward bound mutants behind, he walks past the make-shift bus stop and into the darkness. His cat-like night-vision showing him much more than he cares to see.

Out here in the perimeter, the hand to mouth existence of most mutants was intolerable. With all the materials and labour being allocated exclusively to projects within the confines of the dome, no construction work beyond the initial repairs that were carried out after the apocalypse was sanctioned. The mutated humans had, over time, even come to accept what was left of the quake-ravaged structures. But the inequities even amongst the mutants were intolerable.

The Mutant Council did the best they could to assign living spaces but it was ultimately subject to what was available and not all the mutants had even a wrecked roof to cower under. Many, who couldn't scrape together credits, were forced to live in tents. The fate of senior citizens was particularly deplorable as they had lived out their productive lives and were placed at the bottom of the allocation list. Most had died on the streets.

In the beginning, Josh used to count the number of nights he'd get home without walking by a corpse. Now he simply knew which streets to avoid.

Out of the corner of his eye, he perceives something coming at him. Turning, he distinguishes a mutated animal scampering with three adolescents hot on its tail. *Foragers with torches*, he realizes, *they'd put together from anything dry and combustible they could find.* He knows this because that's how he used to get by. *If they do manage to catch it, they'll have a good meal.* Before his pupils can respond to the sudden burst of light from the flames, the hunters and their prey are long gone.

He is midway between the heavily policed perimeter of the terrarium where the mutant population is near zero and the marketplace teeming with his kind that the remnants of civilization begin to appear.

Picking up his pace, Josh begins ducking into rubble laden alleys, jumping over broken fences and scaling fire escapes which didn't quite transmute—the last of which gets him on the roof of a four-storied building adjacent to a fractured overpass. Backing into one side, he sprints across with all his might and flings himself off the edge.

He had walked by this overpass numerous times and realized

that it would cut his commute short by over thirty minutes. Time he could spend reading. And then he had worked up the courage to jump. The girders that lay bare, splayed out, had nearly carved his left arm open as he tried to get a grip the first time he tried. But now, he lands with practiced ease.

Walking briskly on Interstate 680, he finds himself rubbing shoulders with the mutant populace returning from their day of labour—people he has very limited interaction with.

And soon enough, the survival of the species propaganda, as Dr Hudson puts it, hits him. Blaring from wall-mounted flat-screens that are on—all day, at all main streets at fixed intervals, with the same film on a loop—the United Nation's anthem of hope and survival, a convincing argument to all mankind for symbiotic existence. *Say what you will about the United Nations,* he thinks to himself, *their optics are impeccable.* The words 'Unity amongst the nations brings strength. Strength needed to survive' register, reminding him of the speech the Chief Administrator had once made where he must have quoted that sentence at least a dozen times, while the rest of the discourse comprised of very many adjectives, and very few verbs.

Every now and then he walks past the 'Comply-man'— graffiti of a man in a bio-hazard suit, mask et al, with the word *Comply* incorporated in the design. His fellow mutants seem about as numb as he is to both forms of messaging. He can always tell when a mutant is one of those allowed inside the dome by the purposeful untainted survivor-like stride with which they walk. Those who had been deemed too radioactive to enter the dome usually appeared to move somewhat in slow motion. *Had they given up?* he asks himself. *Had they just accepted their fate in the quarantine zone? Or was that one and the same?*

Catching glimpses of families making do in camp-sites,

impoverished parents putting on brave faces for the young ones scurrying about in oblivious glee, he wonders how the mutant kids spending their first night inside the terrarium must be taking it all. Usually they're just happy to see him at Tweenland on the second day but every once in a while, a child overpowered by cognitive dissonance simply withdraws.

As he makes his way into the marketplace, Josh realizes that he's going to have to kill some time until the crowd thins enough for him to disappear into the basement for the night. No rush though, since the usual falafel roll dinner which he bought from the same street vendor every night had yet to be had. By now, all he had to do was show up and three rolls would be handed over promptly in exchange for the credit card—the one thing every adult, whether untainted human or mutant had been issued by the UN —the great leveller.

But today, the vendor is packing up, and seeing Josh approach says a little sheepishly, "You'll have to go inside the Church, brother. Many parishioners today."

Josh smiles at the thought of seeing Pastor Felipe, because the idea of converting a church and depleted congregation into a successful roll-making business was both admirable and amusing to him at the same time. The pastor preached with just as much conviction as he used to, but the collections that the church made had grown over time due to the food he provided with the faith. The food, of course, had to be paid for and his work-force was compensated with housing and meals only. *Not a bad deal,* Josh muses, *for all parties involved.*

"Welcome to the Lord's house," the Pastor's voice booms across the pewed hall of the still miraculously mostly intact church. "How are you, my son? Still walking in the light, I trust."

"I'm hungry, Pastor," Josh replies with a smile that he hopes doesn't reveal his true feelings at what the good doctor had pointed out to be a shallow pretence.

"Excellent! I have some rolls here and since you've come in, they've been blessed as well," the Pastor rhapsodizes. As Josh approaches politely, head bowed and swipes his card at the collection counter, the entrepreneurial man of the cloth continues, "You should come in more often my son and you shouldn't be coming here alone. I look forward to the day I can solemnize your marriage; it's a sacrament you know. But now that you've taken all this time, take a little more. We're going to carry out renovations and we'll make a grander ceremony out of it."

"Renovations?" Josh asks with genuine curiosity.

"The Lord is kind and the credits are piling up. You're in construction, aren't you?"

Josh nods politely, still waiting for his dinner as Pastor Felipe goes on unabated. "I've even had blue prints drawn up that I'm going to get sanctioned by the Council for Mutant Affairs. Would you like to see them?"

"I only dig holes in the ground, Pastor," Josh replies, his hands clasped, his stomach rumbling. "I wouldn't understand."

"He who tills his land will have plenty of bread," the Pastor quotes scripture as he hands the rolls over. "But take my word for it, our church will be glorious."

97 DAYS AGO: DAY OF REST

8

Philosophy 101

He crawls up to the street before the first light while the marketplace is still deserted, like he does every day. But today he heads in the direction diametrically opposite to the terrarium.

Facing the hills that lie between civilization as it exists and the miles of wasteland that had been cleared, ploughed and turned for agriculture back when the terrarium was being built, he crosses the empty lots and is soon making his way up the high wooden fences that he, unlike the rest of the populace, can scale quite easily.

He could always backtrack just a little in the direction of the terrarium to reach the terminal where rundown and usually overcrowded buses ply various routes in the quarantine zone. Some even take the long way around Mt. Diablo going as far as the edge of the fields, but Josh prefers to save. Besides he has a whole day to fritter away, with little else to do apart from spending quality time with Doc. And he appreciates the change of scenery as well.

He had come across the path to these hills when he had managed to claw his way up the fences by the marketplace for the first time. Having grown weary of the hard life in the quarantine zone, he was trying to run away from it all without a thought as to where he was headed. He was younger back then, easily prone to despair. This was before he had started counsellor training inside the terrarium. Much before he had been found and employed by Mr Sebastian full time.

He ascends the rough terrain quickly over trails discovered across numerous journeys made in the past. He stops at the peak to catch his breath, taking in the sweeping view of Diablo Valley with the terrarium at the horizon; the first rays of the rising sun streaming through the dome, painting the radioactive clouds with hues of pink.

He climbs down just as deftly and makes his way through one plantation after another, purchasing a variety of genetically modified vegetables and grain as he goes along, stuffing and carrying the produce in an oversized jute sack. He doesn't haggle with the farmers, knowing how hard they toil for what little they get due to UN price standardization. By the time the sack is full, his shopping done, he reaches the makeshift bus stop from where he will eventually ride out to Doc's neighbourhood. It's still too early and the bus takes its time to arrive. This being the last stop before the bus turns around to head back to the Quarantine Zone, Josh always gets his choice of seating.

The journey back is long and he nods off, almost missing his stop at Sector 6 in the heart of the Quarantine Zone where Doc lives in what's left of the studio apartment that Josh secured for him when he first found employment.

Being the only survivor from a group of orphans who were treated with an early batch of a radiation protection agent by Dr Hudson, the evaluators from the Mutant Council had worked out a very low survival score for Josh. Had it not been for the accelerated growth, a by-product of his mutation, he would have never made it through the first year. And then there was the good doctor who had watched over him even when they found themselves on the street. This was a debt he was determined to settle.

Lugging the sack of vegetables over his shoulder, he makes his way to the building and is soon knocking on Dr Hudson's door. "Who is it?" comes the familiar raspy voice from within.

"It's me, Doc. Who else would it be?"

Dr Alfred J. Hudson, the former head of Genetics at Stanford, had once been the last word on his subject. Respected by his peers and venerated by his students, he had served as the lead researcher at the Diablo Terrarium—the only mutated scientist on board the United Nations' task force for the final solution.

From the word go, he had lobbied relentlessly for increased concessions for mutants and ruffled quite a few feathers along the way. When he proposed in-utero experimentation to develop a better inoculation, his detractors finally managed to get the better of him claiming his mutation had begun to affect his mind.

What began as mere side-lining soon turned into open antagonism and eventually Dr Hudson was forcibly retired. Classified as an unemployed senior citizen and deemed of little value, the academician was left to die a quiet death.

"You don't look so good, Doc..." Josh remarks, coming face to face with what is left of the once formidable scholar. "Have you begun skipping the antidote again?"

"The antidote?" Dr Hudson scoffs. "You mean the Kool-Aid they've got us all hooked on?"

"Call it what you will," Josh replies, stepping carefully over the fractures in the floor, careful even more, to avert his gaze away from the mutated humans living below. "It's what keeps us going," he adds, as he begins loading up the produce into the corroded fridge he'd purchased from the flea market right after getting his first pay-check from the construction job.

"It keeps us going alright, week after week, back to the hospital for more," Dr Hudson retorts, "where we give up hard earned credits along with our dignity."

"I know Doc, I know," Josh laughs. "Biogenetics industry bad, profiteering yada ya, but it's still all we have."

"So, what have you been reading, son?" Dr Hudson changes the subject of discussion as Josh returns to settle into the only other chair in the dilapidated and crumbling apartment. "I read this really strange book," Josh begins eagerly, "And almost gave up on it because of the way it was written. After struggling with it for a bit, though, I began to start seeing it in my head and that helped. But even after reading and comprehending all that was written, I'm still not sure I understand..."

"What's it called?"

"Waiting for... I'm not sure how to say this..." Josh pauses, "Godot," pronouncing it like 'robot'.

"Waiting for Godot!" Dr Hudson exclaims, his eyes twinkling. "That's an absurdist play from the 1950s, thought to be one of the most significant English plays of the 20th century."

"Play?" Josh blankly echoes. "You mean, like a game?"

"No, no not a game, but theatre. Like a film. An audio-visual presentation. No wonder you found it difficult. In book form, a play contains only the dialogue and stage directions. It takes the presence and talent of actors working towards the vision of a director to make it come alive."

After giving Josh a moment to process this new piece of information, the doctor asks, "So, did you like it?"

"Actually, I don't know what to make of it because from the time it starts and till the time it ends, nothing happens. Not that things don't happen, but Godot," pronouncing it right this time, Josh continues, "keeps them waiting. That's the whole book... play, I mean, and at the end, the humans waiting for Godot start thinking of committing suicide but then the story just ends. At first, I thought the story was about Godot, then I thought it was about the humans or maybe what Godot was going to give them..."

"But that's the whole point," Dr Hudson interjects. "It's about the confrontation of our survival instinct with the meaninglessness of our very existence."

Josh pauses, trying to grasp the insight before continuing haltingly, "Oh... so it's about suicide... yes... Estragon and Vladimir were talking about hanging themselves at the very end..."

"But that didn't happen either," Dr Hudson jumps in again. "Did it?"

"No, they had nothing left to live for, and yet they... That's so depressing..."

"That's existentialism, guised as art," Dr Hudson begins to reminisce, an indulgent smile on his face. "You know, Waiting for Godot was my first brush with philosophy. The ideological piano that landed on my head, back in my sophomore year, all but swayed me to switch my major." As the puzzled look on Josh's face registers on him, the doctor elaborates, "Philosophy is the study of general and fundamental problems concerning matters of existence, knowledge, values, reason and the like. The word itself stands for the love of wisdom."

"Oh!" Josh exclaims. "That sounds really great. Are there any philosophers in the Mutant Council? Or inside the Terrarium? We do have philosophers at the UN, don't we?"

#NOOB PHILOS
I'D LIKE TO THINK SO.. BUT I SUPPOSE THE WORLD CANNOT AFFORD LUXURIES LIKE PHILOSOPHY AT A TIME LIKE THIS.
NOT IN OUR HEMISPHERE, AT LEAST. ALL WE NEED IS THE ANTIDOTE..
YES! WE DO!! WHO CARES! AND MAYBE WATCHING A PLAY ABOUT PEOPLE WITH NOTHING TO LIVE FOR, NOTHING TO LOSE, AND YET BEING UNABLE TO BRING IT ALL TO AN END, WOULDN'T HELP. IT MIGHT EVEN INCREASE SUICIDE RATES IN THE QUARANTINE ZONE.
YES. IT MIGHT. BUT KNOWING THAT WE'VE BEEN DEALING WITH THE ABSURDITY OF OUR EXISTENCE NOT JUST NOW, BUT LONG BEFORE THE PANDEMIC HELPS. DOESN'T IT?
YES DOC, I GUESS YOU'RE RIGHT.

BUT WHERE HAVE THE PHILOSOPHERS GONE? A FEW TAKEN BY THE APOCALYPSE, SOME SILENCED BY THE UNTENABLE POSITIONS THEY HAD ASSUMED. THERE WAS THIS ONE BUFFOON WHO HYPOTHESIZED THAT THERE WAS NO SUCH THING AS HISTORY ANYMORE.
AND THAT TOO DESPITE THE FACT THAT A MAN ENDED UP LEADING A NATION, A MAN WHOSE RACE WAS ENSLAVED, NOT TOO LONG AGO, BY THE VERY NATION THAT HE LED AND REPRESENTED THE WORLD OVER.
ARE YOU REFERRING TO PRESIDENT OBA...
OF COURSE!!
BUT HE WAS JUST A POSTER-BOY. THEY ALL ARE.
WHICH IS NOT TO SAY THAT I QUESTIONED HIS INTENT. HE WAS JUST A LITTLE TOO SMOOTH FOR MY LIKING. AND EVEN IF THAT WASN'T HISTORICAL ENOUGH, I'M SURE THE APOCALYPSE MUST HAVE BEEN.
HMM.. BUT COULD YOU TELL ME MORE ABOUT PHILOSOPHY DOC?
RIGHT... WHERE DO WE BEGIN? SO.. IMAGINE... YOU'RE IN A DARK CAVE, LIKE THIS ROOM WE'RE IN, AND ALL YOU SEE ARE SHADOWS CAST BY OBJECTS AGAINST THE WALL OF THE CAVE. YOU CAN'T SEE THE OBJECTS, REMEMBER, ONLY THE SHADOWS...

"Now if you spent your entire life in this cave, based all your understanding on what you saw, your conclusions would surely be misleading, yes?"

After a moment of reflection, Josh responds, "So, in this cave we're in, the truth is the flame and your thoughts, the shadows?"

"That's one way of looking at it, son." Dr Hudson encourages and, pausing to reflect a little himself, adds quietly, "The truth is, it's all lies." Before Josh can react, he continues, "But going back to the allegory, there's more. One who finds his cherished pre-conceptions and beliefs and values under attack; a fool, as such, would fight to defend them irrespective of how much evidence there is to the contrary. But you're right with my thoughts being the shadows," he admits. "In this situation, where you've received a stripped down vocational education, have no unrestricted access to information—the hive mind, and what with my thoughts being far from infallible..."

"But going back to what I was saying," the good doctor finds his groove again, "Imagine, after a lifetime spent in this cave, you managed to make your way out, saw things for what they were and then returned. Imagine the conversation you'd have with the ones still worshipping the shadows. Imagine how that conversation would end for you."

9

The Immigrant Song

"Ole, ole, ole, ole. Ole... ole..." Tidjane, Kilia's younger sibling whispers in her ear as he pokes her on the shoulder, punctuating each ole.

"Go away, Djane..." she mumbles, clutching her fading dream and turning over.

Yet to go to Tweenland and still unaware of the realities of the world he's born into, Tidjane has restricted access to the terrarium on working days lest he, and others like him, come in contact with mutated humans. Getting impatient, he jostles Kilia, "Wake up!! It's soccer time," and brings out the big guns for good measure, "MAAA! KILIA WON'T WAKE UP... IF WE DON'T LEAVE NOW, I'LL LOSE MY PLACE ON THE TEAM!"

"She's not in Mali, doofus; she's in the other room," Kilia groans.

"AND SHE JUST CALLED ME A DOOFUS!"

Khady, busy gathering clothes for laundry, reluctantly steps in. She appreciates the sacrifice Kilia has made in taking a lesser paying yet more taxing position at the counselling section of Eden (925) just to be close to her family. But she understands the confinement her son is subject to during the workweek as well.

"Kilia, you can nap while Djane is playing can't you?" Khady negotiates.

"Alright, alright, I'm getting up," Kilia sighs, crawling out of bed. "Djane, just give me 15 minutes to freshen up and then we can leave."

"15 MINUTES?!" Tidjane shrieks. "MAA!!!"

"And Djane," Khady reproaches, "don't disrespect your sister by complaining about her all the time."

"We'll do what we want! We'll do what we want! We're Man United! We'll do what we want!" Tidjane echoes the chant of his favourite team's battle-cry as Khady calls out to her husband in the kitchen on her way out. "Alasco, I'm going to the laundromat and then the salon."

"Bye, dear," the well-domesticated head of the Bagyoko household replies as he prepares breakfast for his brood.

"Chew your food properly, dɛnkɛ," Alasco chides, as Tidjane wolfs down soy bread and irradiated eggs from the quarantine zone, treated so as to be fit for human consumption. Turning to his daughter, he adds, "And who's going to eat the eggs I scrambled just for you?" with a doting smile in mock anger.

"You dad, like you always do. C'mon champ, I didn't get up early on my day off for nothing."

As he hears the door close, he begins readying the kitchenette for the baking he's about to do. He had begun out of sheer curiosity brought on by boredom as he waited for Khady to return from her weekly visits to the salon. But over time, he got better, and the aroma of freshly baked goodies always got his wife in just the right mood.

When Khady returns, resplendent in a hair-do that's a beautiful fusion of the Malian type that Alasco prefers and some trimmings of the Western styles that he is slowly coming to accept, she glows from the herbal facial treatments. And seeing her like this, Alasco rises with hunger in his eyes. Smiling knowingly, Khady turns her head side to side with a, "No, Alasco, I got a mani-pedi today as well, and that took more time. The champ and your daughter will be back soon."

"Cɛɲi masamuso, why do you make me suffer..." Alasco flirts, hoping for a little treat. "Alasco..." Khady starts, veering away off a tangent. "Do you realize you've become more Malian now than you ever were while we were still in Mali?"

"Maybe you're right, dear," Alasco parries, trying to steer the conversation back. "I'm happy we're living well, earning our keep, but what good is it if we don't enjoy the..."

"Of course, I'm right!" Khady explodes. "Look at the life Djane has ahead of him. And do you think Kilia would've received the education she did at Columbia if we were still back home?"

"Of course she wouldn't, Khady," Alasco responds, his heart now doing the talking, stemming Khady's sudden outburst. "But I worry that growing up in this place Tidjane will know nothing about the land and the legends of his people. It was bad enough that Kilia could spend only so much time with the family in the village but that was better than this. And what of her marriage?"

Just then they hear the door open and Tidjane runs inside screaming excitedly, "WE WON! WE WON!"

"All the games you played today, Djane?" Khady asks, swelling with pride.

"Yes, Ma. The teams and my mates were shuffled, but I was on the winning side for all of them."

Just then, Kilia's iPad makes the sound her parents know all too well. "Mmm... something smells good! Is it ready?" she asks, eyes glued to the screen.

"Yes, dear, it is," Alasco replies. "And see how beautiful your mother looks today."

"Wow, mom," Kilia exclaims, turning to her mother, iPad raised instinctively as Khady protests in memory of the styling accident she had inflicted upon her daughter, leaving once tender hair streaked with rivulets of white. "Not that narcissism again," Khady adds, recovering quickly. "Come, come, let's see what your father's been up to."

"So Kilia," Khady asks between mouthfuls of soy stew, "how are your friends? Any of them getting married—any of the still single ones, I mean." Ever thankful for the credits she earns from her counselling assignment and the help with housework she gets, Khady, like any mother, longs to see her daughter betrothed.

Kilia keeps eating in silence, a dark look crossing her face.

"You know, Kilia, if you don't want to move away from us, you can always get enrolled in the dating registry of the Diablo Terrarium," Alasco adds, trying to be helpful. "I think you can do it on that hand computer of yours. I don't mean to pressure you, but we have an old saying—*If you've nothing to do, dig a spinster's grave.*"

Tidjane, oblivious to the shift in the atmosphere, chews noisily as Kilia puts her spoon to rest on the plate and glares at her father.

"Or you could come with me and Djane to the socials for people of African origin..." Alasco says, his voice trailing off.

"We are a one-world nation now, Alasco," his wife states matter-of-factly, picking one of the assorted cookies her husband has laid out. "Our girl doesn't have to settle for a

Malian, or even an African boy. Mmm... white-chocolate raisin cookies."

"Settle for?" Alasco's whisper reverberates with betrayal.

"Settle with... I meant settle with... Kilia can settle with anyone she likes."

"Dad! Mom! Please! We've been over this!" Kilia exclaims, holding up both hands in resignation. Tidjane looks up from his plate, his attention snagged, but keeps eating just the same.

After lunch is over and Khady has taken charge of the kitchen again, Alasco instructs his son, "Better get cleaned up denkɛ, we should be leaving soon," as he sets off to ready himself. He always wears one of his Bògòlanfini full-length tunics for these things, knowing that this is about the only time when his son can truly learn what it means to be a Malian.

At the social, as often is the case, there are a few new arrivals. And today, there's one who's introducing himself just as the father and son walk in. "The Sur-13 Vatos drove by, homies got shot. I was just a bitch-ass punk smokin' a sherm stick on the block when it all went down... Saw the blood on me... knew it was time to *represent.*" Unable to make sense of a single word he's heard so far, Alasco begins scanning the reactions of those around.

"My boys at 30 deep started me off with a Hi-Point... When I was done sending a dozen cholos to *Hey-soos,*" the new arrival mocks the Latino accent, "Keon showed me his respect with a Glock. Na'mean! But dem real niggas, I met at the penitentiary." The discomfort on the faces of everyone at the social is painfully evident and Alasco steals a glance at his son, making a mental note to have a discussion with Khady.

But first I'll have to figure out what this wildly gesticulating man is saying, he thinks to himself.

And, to his relief, the group moderator steps in. "Why don't you tell us about how you embraced Islam, brother. I'm sure everyone would like to know."

"Aight. Dem real Niggas, some of 'em was Muslim. When Prisoner No. 95095, Waliyy Abdur Rahim, or as you may know him—Hook Mitchell—hollered at me that I started to listen. *Damn that nigga can jump!* After seeing him on court, I'd have believed anything that came outta his mouth. But all he said was Allah be purifying him for his bad choices. It don't matter if society or the judge was wrong. *The real judge will reward our faith on the day of judgement.*"

"Ameen..." the Imam declares softly, as the moderator continues helping the former convict along, "And how do you like it here?"

"I won't lie, it ain't easy. Holdin' down a factory job ain't nuttin, but keeping up the good behaviour... sometimes I look me in the mirror and think I'm frontin. Or maybe this place be just another big-assed prison with rules and shit, just the guards don't beat on your ass for every little thang. It's good to be here with my brothers, na'mean. Seeing white-boy-blue-eyes-on-the-cross every Sunday didn't do nuttin, but praying to Allah five times a day keeps it real, ya *feel* me?"

"Ameen!" the Imam declares again, his congregation echoing whole heartedly. Alasco follows suit, still a little unsure of what he is affirming. "Thank you for sharing, brother," the moderator says, getting a nod from the Imam. "It's time for the Asr-Salah."

As the Azaan is recited, everyone rises and turns towards Mecca.

After the supplications, light refreshments are served buffet style, and the attendees get to circulate and mingle. This being Mali's time to shine, Alasco turns to his son with a smile and whispers, "Pay attention as I speak to the elders, Djane. That's the only way to learn."

10

A Gentleman's Agreement

David steps nervously out of the decontamination chambers and into the terrarium. It's not so much that he is here in violation of protocol—no mutants are allowed inside on the day of rest but then again, he's here at the Chief Administrator's behest—as it is that the request to meet was delivered via non-official channels and confidentiality was implied which unsettles him.

Even before he can get his bearings, a strapping young peacekeeper standing by a standard delivery van calls out in a thickly accented voice, "Mr Cohen?"

"Yes, I am David Cohen..."

"Please come with me, sir!" the obviously well-trained peacekeeper says, leading David to the back of the van. Opening the door, he waits as his charge boards the vehicle and follows him inside. "Before we go any further, I must ask you to put this on, sir," the peacekeeper says, handing David a small package. Forcing a smile as he takes and opens the package, but not knowing what to do with the black sheets inside, David turns tentatively to his escort.

"It's a burqua, Mr Cohen. Here, let me help."

David manages to read his escort's name off the badge sewn onto his uniform as he is assisted in wearing the two-piece outfit that covers him from head to toe.

"Thank you, Jan."

The peacekeeper breaks into a broad grin and replies, "It's nothing, Mr Cohen." Turning to the man in the driver's seat, Jan speaks through the sliding window as he raps his knuckles sharply on it, "We're good, let's go."

The garment of modesty is a little stifling but David finds comfort in the obscurity it affords. "Is that a Danish accent?" he ventures.

"Ja, Mr Cohen. How did you know? Have you been to Denmark?"

"Yes, I've spent quite some time in Copenhagen, in Christiania, in fact."

"You've been to Fristaden!" Jan can barely contain his excitement. "I used to go there a lot with my high school friends. When we wanted to, you know..."

"Get high?" David finishes the sentence with a knowing smile.

Seeing the colour rise up in Jan's face, David quickly adds, "I've spent my fair share of time at Pusher Street too," putting the young man at ease once again. "We were there filming a documentary after the 2005 incident and it was hard not to be seduced by the pacifistic freethinking of the anarchist commune."

Sensing that the socio-politics of it all was lost on the young Dane, David asks the peacekeeper what he misses the most about home. The answer, not surprisingly, is the food. And the culinary journey that Jan takes off on lasts them until the van finally comes to a halt.

Not used to wearing a burqua, David trips as he is disembarking and nearly falls when Jan steadies him. After taking one last look to make sure both the disguise and the man within are in order, Jan briefs David. "We're inside a delivery bay in the basement of Tower Twelve. We'll ride the freight elevator to Level 3 and take the commuter elevator from there to the Club Level. That's where *he* is waiting for you. Follow me and say nothing until we get there. Tap my shoulder if you must speak and I'll come close enough for you to whisper in my ear. Alright then, let's go."

From the moment they alight the freight elevator on the third level, David begins to feel a sense of familiarity with the environs. It is a while before it dawns upon him but standing on the walkalator, about halfway between the hypermarket where they emerged and the central elevator bay that they are headed towards, David realizes that the place is much like an airport terminal.

The citizens in and around the supermarket, much like passengers in a duty-free lounge, mill about seeming to enjoy the time they are killing. The uniformed staff, whether they are stocking shelves, manning counters, scurrying about with carts loaded with cleaning equipment in tow, or politely enforcing order and maintaining decorum; they all do their jobs with an air of detached pleasantness.

The walkalators themselves start and end where smaller corridors meet the large one they are passing through. And the multilingual directional signs, markings and graphics almost seem to beckon towards boarding gates. All that's missing are the controlled announcements about arrivals and departures.

Jan has a short but friendly exchange with one of the peacekeepers overseeing the central elevator bay while they wait. On the way there, David had noticed a few citizens in what could only be described as exotic attire. But even so, he isn't exactly inconspicuous in the burqua. The peacekeeper whom Jan is talking to, however, doesn't appear to notice him at all and cheerily waves them on when the elevator arrives.

Fifteen stories later, still silently following his escort, David emerges at the Club Level. As the group of teenagers who had all but begun playing football while still riding the elevator with them head straight to the reception counter, Jan leads David to the staff entrance.

Upon seeing them, the young lady manning the desk straightens in her chair and whispers conspiratorially, "*He* is at the squash courts in Section C. You know the way, right?"

"Ja!" the peacekeeper responds and leads David all the way in.

Extending his hand with a jaunty smile that goes well with his sporty attire, the Chief Administrator welcomes David. "We have the section to ourselves, Councilman, I'm sure you're dying to get out of that stifling burqua." Sensing David's nervousness from his tentative grip, the Chief Administrator continues, "I trust you had no trouble getting here, David."

"No trouble at all, Chief Administrator," David answers, lifting the veil covering his face to reveal a relieved smile. "Jan took good care of me."

"He takes good care of me too. Don't you, Jan?"

The peacekeeper smiles stiffly as he stands in attention, waiting to be dismissed.

"That will be all, Jan. Please wait for us by the entrance." As Jan clicks his heels and marches off, the Chief Administrator turns to David with a perfunctory "Shall we?" and points to the changing rooms.

The set of colour coordinated t-shirt, track pants and shoes that David finds in there are a rather good fit. Clearly the Chief Administrator had gone all out and the delighted surprise on David's face when he sees his host with squash rackets is less than sincere.

"I hear you were a varsity squash sensation," the Chief

Administrator says, alluding to the file he has on David.

"It's been a while since I've played," David replies, evading his host's gambit. "I don't know if I'll be any good, but I sure will enjoy the game."

"Did you let me win, Davie?" the Chief Administrator asks abruptly, as they are relaxing in the sauna.

"Oh no, Chief." Somewhere during the game, as comfort set in, they had begun calling each other Davie and Chief. "I just couldn't keep up with you. Were you a competitive player in your student days as well?"

"I wasn't much of anything back then, I must confess. I didn't know who I was, or what I wanted to do. And like so many privileged and aimless youngsters, I decided to go around the world in search of myself."

"Is that how you ended up in Thailand?" David asks, slipping into the role of charmed listener.

"Precisely," the Chief Administrator replies. "I grew a little too fond of that place and even took up odd jobs to sustain myself when my father, in an attempt to force me back home, cut me off."

"You worked your way up to running a world standard resort from a daily-wager!" David exclaims, his admiration genuine this time.

"It wasn't all that bad, Davie. The first McDonald's had just opened up in Bangkok and the manager saw value in having a white teenager behind the counter at the all-American burger joint."

"He sounds like a smart man," David reflects as he reclines on the wooden bench to keep the Chief Administrator going.

"That he was. Most outsiders, especially us westerners, don't give the Thai enough credit. Did you know they were the only people in South East Asia able to resist colonization?" Noting the look of surprise on David's face with satisfaction, the Chief Administrator continues sagaciously, "They're a very unique people, the Thai. And there is much to be learnt from them."

"Could you share an insight, perhaps?" David asks after just the right amount of time has passed, snapping the Chief Administrator out of his reverie.

"Give others whatever they desire. Without judgment. Whilst keeping up appearances, and you will never be questioned."

"Whoa... that sounds pretty Machiavellian, Chief," David slips up.

"I'm no fancy college boy like you, Davie," the Chief Administrator responds with mild amusement. "I didn't even understand what you just said but I know people. Preferences may vary, but ultimately, we all want the same thing. Bliss. As we define it. That's where the variances come to play. Judgment always gets in the way. But our bliss, whatever it is, is all we seek. Let's hit the showers. I'd like to take you to my quarters and share some wine and cheese."

"The night has a thousand eyes?" David asks, the delight audible in his voice, less than five seconds into the track.

"I had no idea you were a jazz hound," the Chief Administrator nods in affirmation as he speaks.

"No, no, it's not that. In film school, for one of our projects, we had to cut a video of ourselves cooking an egg to a jazz song of our choice. I randomly chose this one, and well, ended up listening to it for four hours or so at the editing table."

The wine was loosening his tongue and David, sensing his seduction being in its final stages keeps talking. "Wish to hate a song? Use it as your score," he adds, for good measure.

"I see. Something else, then." the Chief Administrator says, rising towards the wall-mounted entertainment console.

As a recursive beat, synthesized sounds, repetitive lyrics delivered by heavily auto-tuned vocals fill the living room, the Chief Administrator walks over to the wall-sized windows. And though he can't see beyond the perimeter of the terrarium, he stands there gazing into the distant darkness. "I worry for our people in the quarantine zone, Davie. I worry because my work keeps me here at all times. For the life of me, I can't remember the last time I was out there."

But David does.

That was the day the Chief Administrator had arrived to take up his post at Eden (925). And hadn't set foot out ever since.

"By the way, Rolfe was moved by the film you shot for us."

"Thank you, Chief."

"As I was saying, Davie, I worry for our people. I wish I could show them how much we care. If only I could stand there on the streets, like those screens that play the U.N. anthem, to let them know that no matter what comes to pass, we're all in it together."

"Um... Chief..." David begins, mouthing words that have all but been written for him. "How about a series of 'fire-side chats'? You've got us a camera already and the broadcast system is in place as it is."

"Genius, Davie, that's pure genius!"

"I can't believe you live so modestly, Chief," David says as he dabs his mouth with the napkin. "The first citizen of a terrarium and all you take for yourself is a studio apartment?"

"I don't need much to get by," the Chief Administrator says, waving the Spartan quarters away. "What little I save, I spend on wine and cheese and they don't take up too much space. I hope you enjoyed today's selection." He pauses, smiles reflectively and continues, "What about loved ones, Davie, any of yours out there? In here? Or do you, like me, stand alone?"

"There was someone; we were to marry. She serves as a news announcer for one of the terrariums in Australia," comes the terse reply.

"She must be a looker. Or was she a mouthpiece? Either way, good for you," the Chief Administrator remarks, blithely glossing over the divides, both geographical and biogenetic. "Was she your muse, then, in your directorial days?"

As David takes a sip of wine to steady himself, the Chief Administrator continues, "I don't want to get ahead of myself here, but we just might be able to have her transferred back. And as a special liaison, you could visit her on every day of rest. Not just on the days you come to play squash with me. You'd have to keep wearing that burqua, of course, and be accompanied by Jan at all times but we just might be able to work something out."

"Special liaison?" David mumbles in response.

"Don't worry about the title, Davie, it'll be strictly off the record. Only a trusted few will know of your visits and not a soul shall know about our arrangement." As the Chief Administrator prattles on euphemistically, David's thoughts turn to the love of his life. She had taken the red-eye to the East coast the night before the apocalypse and never returned. Choosing a camera facing position on another continent over a lesser job at Eden (925), she had made her priorities clear.

"You strike me as a pragmatic," the Chief Administrator says, gently placing his hand on David's arm. "Unlike some of the others on the Mutant Council. As my newly appointed special liaison, what can you tell me about the 'comply' graffiti that has been popping up all over the quarantine zone?"

84

#Stalkward   **Follow** •••

It's amazing how much they do with the regulation gabardine over at Zara. I don't know how long it'll be before I can save up enough credits to buy something outside the UN templates, something designer. But there's no charge for trying stuff on and taking selfies, amirite? In the good ole days we had a return policy as well. But whatevs!

As I was leaving the store, I thought I saw someone familiar. When I called out, he began rushing away and ended up on the floor under a pile of their new arrivals xD

He was the last person I'd expect to see there and seeing him squirm, I was all *aww* in my head, so I asked if he'd like to get a cup of coffee. I got into work mode, I guess, and asked what I could bring him. But he insisted on doing the courteous gent thing. This time I Awwed Out Loud. *blushes and runs away*

The n00b really likes green tea *facepalm*

When I asked him what he did off work, William went on some 'rate of diffusion for a concept' trip; I should Google that or whatever. After giving me like a 15-minute speech on memes *(duh!)* full of ginormous words like 'freedom of speech,' 'social commentary' and 'collective something,' he asked if I understood.

And when I went, 'yea, you write jokes', he turned as red as my blush lipstick. Not just on his cheeks. But all over and that's when I knew he'd totes lost it.

I didn't mean to kill his buzz or whatever but it took forever for him to calm down. It was good to see a glimpse of the real him tho. And all this while I thought he was an Android. Poor thing, I've seen him hovering around the cafeteria. It's like he's a little puppy, figuring out how to talk, walk, and blend in. He doesn't realize how transparent he is xD!

And yea, I didn't bump into the Big Chief today either. Another 4 hours at Tower Twelve wasted. I wonder what he does with himself on his days off.

11

Viva La Évolution!

"Are we sure we want to do this?" the tall surgeon asks, looking first at the others with him in the operation theatre, then at those seated in the viewing gallery as a cadaver lies, slowly decomposing, on the operating table.

This pretence wouldn't hold up to anything more than a cursory examination, but it does afford a venue they can all visit regularly without arousing the slightest suspicion.

Most of those present avert their gaze from the tall surgeon who has verbalized a doubt which none of them wish to admit. Hands are wrung, clothing is adjusted. One of those present in the gallery takes off his glasses and starts polishing the lens.

For a while, no one says anything. Then, the high spirited young lady seated next to the seemingly disinterested tattooed man counters, "Is our situation not compelling enough for you?" Her voice getting shriller and her tone more heated as she goes on. "Did you not pass through the same corridors as we did when we walked in here today? Are you even one of us or..."

"Aiko Chan!" the young lady's companion says softly and she slumps back in her seat, her voice trailing off mid-sentence.

"The suffering of our kind is not lost upon me," the man in the operation theatre replies, unfazed. "If I didn't feel as you do, I wouldn't be here. I only ask because we're crossing the point of no return here."

"So we put matter to vote again—all in favour!" the young lady's companion shoots back, with just a trace of scorn in the otherwise cool smile on his face and starts raising his hand.

"No, no, there's no need for that," the surgeon interrupts, still courteous, still gentle. "As long as we understand the consequences..."

"Now all we need to do is figure out how to acquire the supplies we need in order to carry out the plan and we can be on our way," the portly gent in the gallery who had so far busied himself fastidiously cleaning his spectacles declares, placing them back on his face.

"Yes, that's actually what bothers me more than anything else," another participant, also dressed in scrubs says, "since we need not just gasoline, but a specific ingredient which simply isn't available."

"Relax, doctor, I know man who have interest in someone on our side of the fence," the tattooed man replies nonchalantly. "I have been cultivating him for some time. I give him right kind of motivation, he get us all we need."

"And what, exactly, are we going to offer this man you speak of?" the tall surgeon asks.

The tattooed man answers brusquely without skipping a beat, "Don't you wonder how we get to meet in here?" Pausing just long enough for his question to take hold, he continues, "One of us have connection that go all way up to Mutant Council."

Everyone turns to stare at him but he continues unabashedly, "I not be surprised if one of us is directly connected to Council, maybe Councilman even."

All eyes in the viewing gallery immediately turn towards the participants in the theatre, their forms obscured by the scrubs and their faces hidden behind masks and caps, with emotions ranging from suspicion to a grudging respect as none of them has ever seen any of the five without the masquerade.

The oppressive silence that follows yields only when the portly gent noisily clears his throat, following it up with a stiff, "If that is all, I suppose we can wrap this meeting. Be well everyone," and rises hastily to leave.

One of those dressed in scrubs, a lady who hasn't said a word during the course of the entire discussion concludes the meeting. "You'll be notified about our next meet when you come in to get your dose of the antidote." Raising her fist to shoulder level, her elbow by her hip, she adds, "For Évolution!"

As the participants echo the refrain and make their way out of the viewing gallery, she covers the lifeless body on the operating table, unclasps the locks on the wheels of the gurney and carts it off. Two of the surgeons follow her out, leaving the tall man who did most of the talking and the one whom the tattooed man had referred to as 'Doctor' to their devices.

"You don't think he knows who we are, do you?" the tall man asks, a little concerned.

"No, Councilman," the other replies. "I'm sure it's just bravado, an educated guess, perhaps. And when he called me 'Doctor,' it was sarcasm. Although I find the irony rather amusing."

"Yes, you're probably right," the tall man replies. "I give him too much credit. He betrays his recklessness in trying to appear to know more than he actually does. But then again, it's his recklessness that makes him so valuable."

89 DAYS AGO:
VISA, VISITATION RIGHTS, DEAD BABIES.

12

Trading Faces

After securing the protective shoes and gloves to the biohazard suit, the decontamination unit technician fits the headgear on the Deputy Chief Administrator and tests its integrity as if he were going out into the Quarantine Zone himself.

By the time No. 2 is accoutred, he finds Miss Paige, similarly outfitted, awaiting him with his security escort. Seeing No. 2 shaking hands wherever he goes and with whomever he meets, the young blonde asks, "Do you, like, know everyone in the terrarium, No. 2?"

"I'm just good with faces, Miss," the Deputy replies with a smile and a child-like wink. "Besides, the technicians here, I see them every fortnight, so..."

As the van pulls up, the Deputy Chief turns to Paige, "Would you like to sit in the front, this being your first visit and everything?"

"Oh that would be awesome!" Paige exclaims, hopping in. "But I'm a little freaked out after all I saw in the film which Councilman David made."

"Don't worry, Miss," the Deputy Chief Administrator assures. "You've already seen the worst, and besides, you're going to have to face it sooner or later."

"So, you were planning on joining the peace corps before the apocalypse?" No. 2 engages Paige in small talk, sensing her growing discomfort by the time they are halfway into the Quarantine Zone.

"Yes, No. 2. How'd you guess?"

"William told me. He must have, how you say, read it in your personnel file."

"My file?" getting a little self-conscious, she turns around to face the Deputy Chief Administrator and continues in a somewhat subdued tone. "So, um, does he have access to, like, everyone's files?"

"*Si*, of course. He's the Administrative Associate. And not just files, but access to all records, areas, everything. As he should. He's being groomed to be a Chief Administrator, maybe even more."

"No way!" she exclaims again, now just a little delighted.

"Good, *si?*" No. 2 rejoins, winking again.

When they get to their destination, they find David waiting by the rubble encrusted entrance. The chambers of the Mutant Council they may be, but they are no better than the rest of the Quarantine Zone.

"*Hola* David," No. 2 begins, as Paige slowly, and with just a little uncertainty, steps out onto the scorched earth. "I'm sure you remember the Chief Administrator's assistant, it's her first time outside so..."

"Yes, of course," David responds enthusiastically, "Welcome, Miss Paige," turning to her, hand extended.

Somewhat reconstructed on the inside, the chambers of the Mutant Council have air-conditioning with detoxification filters for when officials from the Terrarium visit. The members of the Mutant Council rise as the Deputy Chief walks in with David and Paige in tow even though No. 2

always got embarrassed by this show of respect. After taking off his headgear but instructing Paige not to, he begins pleasantly, *"Cómo estás,* my fellow office-bearers." Humbly he adds, "Please sit," as he himself takes his designated seat at the head of the table.

"Gentlemen, since you may be wondering, we have Miss Paige here with us today. She assists the Chief Administrator, you see, and we can upload the updates to her iPad today instead of mine. Before we begin, anything out of the ordinary?" No. 2 inquires hopefully, because most of the news that comes from the Quarantine Zone is as painful to him as it is bad. Despite his years of living amidst and dealing with suffering as a veteran UN volunteer, the horrors of this apocalypse are sometimes too much even for him.

The Councilman overseeing the animal population leans forward and begins rambling enthusiastically, "I have some great news, No. 2. I'm not sure if this trend will sustain but our surveyors have noted a resurgence of certain flora and fauna. Even some species heading towards extinction appear to be resurging. We'll keep observing, of course, until we can say for sure."

"Such is the power of nature," the Chief Councilman is quick to add, not wishing to be left out of the conversation. "It has the ability to heal itself." Continuing ruefully, he concludes, "If only we humans could do the same."

"What about death rates, Chief Councilman?" No. 2 asks, an imperceptible quaver in his voice, to get past the worst as quickly as he can.

"Death rates?" Paige blurts from the corner where she's perched, unable to contain herself.

"I'll explain later Miss Paige. Remember, you're here only to observe," No. 2 rebukes gently.

The Chief Councilman seems a little miffed as he answers,

"Deputy Chief, they're more or less the same, but we really need a better antidote; the mutation in some seems to be developing a resistance to the medication."

"I'll convey your concerns up along the chain of command and I'll speak to Dr DeChampeaux as well."

To Paige, this meeting with the Mutant Council chaired by No. 2 is reminiscent of, but in stark contrast with, the weekly meets she is accustomed to back at the Terrarium. The atmosphere here is relaxed, the mood is friendly. And before she knows it, the meet comes to an end. "*Excelente*! Looks like we've covered everything," the Deputy Chief Administrator remarks. "*Pero*, how is Dr Hudson?"

A brief stillness descends over the entire Council and for a moment, all that can be heard is the whirring of the air-conditioning.

"That stupid boy insists on keeping the man alive," the Chief Councilman breaks the silence acrimoniously. "And that crazy old coot continues to rabble-rouse with those who still cling to him." David nods at No. 2, a reassuring smile on his face to convey that all is well, and begins rising from his seat, in conclusion.

"Why don't you talk to some of the Councilmen, Miss Paige," No. 2 instructs, slowly rising, "while I see to my meetings from the outreach program." As he starts following David out of the chambers of the council, he adds awkwardly, "Thank you for your service, fellow volunteers."

As they make their way to one of the smaller chambers, David whispers, "He's become quite a reclusive and bitter old coot," with a muffled laugh. "And he does tend to attract subversive elements. I've got my eye on him though, and it's all mostly harmless." Opening the door, he announces, "Your first meet today is with Viktor, one of Dr Hudson's regulars."

As they enter, they see Viktor sitting a little too comfortably, considering he has been summoned to meet the Deputy Chief Administrator of the UN Mission out of the blue. He is leaning back, legs crossed, one arm hitched over the chair, tattoos on full display. He doesn't rise or even sit up when David and No. 2 step in.

"Viktor, this is the Deputy Chief," David opens.

To ease the tension in the air, No. 2 adds, "All formalities aside, Viktor, please tell us what we can do for you."

Viktor bristles a little, but replies with a cool, "Have everything we need." As he nods unceremoniously at David he adds, "He call me. I come."

"Yes, Viktor, of course," David mutters, but continues respectfully. "Let me introduce you properly, and outline the agenda for today's discussion." Turning to the Deputy Chief Administrator, David begins officiously again, but this time just a little softer, "No. 2, Viktor originally immigrated from Russia years ago. He is a prominent street artist. After the Kremlin took note of his work he sought, and was granted, asylum here."

"That is ancient history, Councilman," Viktor cuts in abruptly. "I work as gold-digger in cash-cow industry of Quarantine Zone. And on side, I make and sell Krokodil."

"Oh, I see the Russian connection now," No. 2 murmurs. Remembering in a flash what fellow volunteers from Russia had once pointed out during missions in Africa before the apocalypse—they have no *the* in their grammar. "It's not just *Rasha* no more," Viktor keeps going. "We die for it. Chernobyl, yes?" casting a deathly glance at No. 2. "Now Krokodil variants being made in quarantine zones across world as source of relief to my kind."

"We are all still human, Viktor," No. 2 interjects, but Viktor wordlessly crosses his arms across his chest. The spark in his eyes now lacking the kindle.

"No one's denying the need for concessions like Krokodil anymore," David soothes. "The market isn't regulated and no sanctions or prohibitions have been placed either."

"Of course not! There is only one product. One service. One cause and one end. Mutants need no more reason to rise against oppression of humanity, no?"

"Yes, Viktor," David concedes. "As a fellow mutant, I see what you're saying but we have called you in because you're a celebrity in what's left of the counter-cultural community in the greater Diablo area..."

"Oh!" Viktor exclaims, finally beginning to thaw. "So you want to discuss Biohazard Man?"

"Yes, Viktor, exactly!" David replies, the relief evident on his face.

"Oh, they just kids," Viktor preens. "I don't know where they find paint, but they young, want to express. They come to me, ask if I want to join. But the artwork is homage to Shepard Fairey's 'Obey' piece." Seeing the blank looks on David and No. 2's faces, he explains. "The one where he used the face of *Andre the Giant* as the underlying graphic. Don't you see face-value? Recognition? Recall? How we say in art, post-post-modern sign and signification."

"You know you're always in my prayers, right?" No. 2's second meet doesn't seem to be going any better than his first. "Of course, pastor, of course," he replies gratefully. "You may not be a congregant, Jorge," the minister continues, "but you are my parishioner just the same."

"Pastor Felipe has a proposal that we've turned down repeatedly, citing Section 14, clause B of the UN Charter, but I've scheduled this meeting at his insistence, No. 2," David rushes through, knowing how hard it is to get a word in when the pastor is present.

"Yes David. You did. Now could I have a word with the Deputy Chief in private?" And turning to No. 2, Pastor Felipe pronounces without a care, "One who speaks in a tongue edifies himself; but one who prophesies edifies the church," before David has left.

"He's a good man, Pastor..." No. 2 begins after David has closed the door behind him, only to be interrupted immediately. "No Jorge, you are. Even when you lie to uphold a fallen soul, the truth speaks for itself on your face." The preacher continues, "So also you, since you are zealous of spiritual gifts, seek to abound for the edification of the church."

"Corinthians?"

"Very good, my son," Pastor Felipe replies softly. "How I wish you would come to our Church on the Sabbath. But knowing it's a working day for you, I understand."

"Your proposal, Pastor?" No. 2 asks tentatively.

"Our church attained 'conference' status a while ago, thanks to His Grace and the devotion of the faithful." Noting No. 2 cross himself with satisfaction, Pastor Felipe continues, booming again, as he unrolls the blue-prints and lays them out on the table. "According to the grace of God which was given to me, like a wise master builder I laid a foundation, and another is building on it. But each man must be careful how he builds on it."

13

Visitation Rights

"Today, kids, is the day you get to see the Terrarium in its entirety," Kilia says, starting the day off at Tweenland. "But before we go exploring, let me tell you a little about where I'm from. My parents and I, we came here from Mali, which is far away from here."

"It's in Africa, on another continent," Poo pipes up, knowingly.

"Exactly," Kilia resumes. "So we don't have terrariums there. At least not yet."

"Nor a quarantine zone," Josh chimes in, on cue.

"We used to live in a tightly knit community in a village," Kilia continues, "where everyone knew everyone else and the whole village was one big family. Life was rough, as it can sometimes be in the quarantine zone, but we had vast open spaces, we played games. Told and heard stories. There was always enough for everyone because we asked so little of each other…"

"Just like we're doing now in this camp, kids." Josh says quickly, anxious as always, whenever Kilia strays off-script and adds, "Let's go, kids!" for good measure.

"I can't see, I can't see!" one of the untainted human kids

cries, as they stand around a scale model of the terrarium in the atrium of the counselling centre. The tour for the children always starts here and it is Josh's job to get them all in place.

"Alright, children, so this here is the terrarium we're in," Kilia begins her monologue. "Let me tell you a little about the architect, Rem Koolhaas, who designed it, and his quest—*to keep thinking about what architecture could be, what he could be.* As he saw it, we're all like bees living in this hive. There's no queen, of course. We're all volunteers, living and working together to help the mutated humans living alongside us. So, we'll see hexagons everywhere, just like we do on beehives. And the occasional pentagon to hold it all together. Like the traditional football pattern of yesteryears. The architect made a strong argument for his designs based on the same."

"What's a hexagon?" Poo asks.

"A six-sided shape," Josh replies, pointing at one of the panes that make up the little glass dome. "And as you'll see, they're a recurring motif."

"Initially," Kilia resumes, "another architect, a lady of middle-eastern origin operating from Europe, was to design our terrariums for us. But her style was deemed too eccentric. Many thought one of her projects, a stadium, looked like a vagina."

"Vagina!" one of the mutant kids exclaims, eliciting a range of reactions from the children.

"Calm down, kids," Josh steps in again. "We've been over all this in our anatomy session last week and by now, you're old enough to know and use those words."

"So, the terrarium has a diameter of 16.7 km," Kilia rattles off, a little unsure of whether the children can grasp these spatial concepts. "The monorail the mutated children rode in on," Kilia points at the little train on tracks in the scale model as she speaks, "on your first day here, from the decontamination zone—the only way in and out of the terrarium to the counselling centre—is about half the diameter of the terrarium as it has been laid out on that one side only, for now."

"What are those?" one of the children asks, pointing at the grey structures along the monorail tracks. "Good, I was just coming to that," Kilia replies. "Those are manufacturing units where we make a whole range of goods and products. There are the plastic industries with attached recycling units. And a whole section dedicated to electricals and electronic goods where assembly and maintenance takes place. Since soy is our staple, soy preparations such as milk, cheese, butter and bread are produced there as well."

"We have manufacturing industries on the outside too," Josh adds, taking ownership of all quarantine zone related information as he always does. "Paper from all the wood pulp that is brought in on the railways which connect us to the as yet unaffected areas of the world is processed there. In fact, all the industries that rely on imported raw materials such as fabrics, assembled appliances, furniture and plumbing fixtures—among others are all with us on the outside."

"Running everything with clock-work precision for us inside the dome," Kilia says, taking the lead again, "is a central A.I. brain with sensors operating doors in all public spaces and load balancing the elevators, walkalators, the monorail and the public transport buses for the use of volunteers and mutated humans alike." Pausing briefly to catch her breath, she continues, "We also have an automated garbage disposal system and a recycling plant, with round the clock power and clean water, thanks to our waterworks and water recycling plants. The power comes from the electricity generation plant and the six Tesla substations," Kilia says, as she points at the golden points of the hexagon that lie outside the tower complex.

"Much like the substations we have out in the Quarantine Zone as well," Josh adds, glad to see the smiles reappearing on the faces of the awed mutant kids. One of them seems a little disturbed though. He looks up to Josh saying, "This is Camelot, but only for them."

"Don't think of this as a juxtaposition of an emerald city and a ghetto, sweetie," Kilia soothes. "There are downsides of living here too. You have space, open spaces that someone like me longs for, and you have to understand, all of us UN volunteers—and that means everyone who lives in this terrarium—is making a sacrifice to be here with you... right? But most of all, we are in constant danger of exposure to radiation and fall-out. A few volunteers have suffered from mutation themselves and now live amongst you as they continue to help. Remember Shanice's father?"

"Besides," Josh adds, improvising, "this social order isn't going to last forever. Someday, when the radiation levels have subsided enough to dismantle the dome and open up the Terrarium, we'll all live as one."

"Now let me tell you about the spire in the middle with the structures at its top," Kilia says, pointing to the needle shaped edifice in the dead centre of the dome. "That there is the Administrative Office which is hexagon shaped too. Several hexagons in fact, one over the other, diminishing in size from the top to the bottom. The lower-most one is where the Chief Administrator's office and the conference room are located. A vantage point that allows him to see all that goes on inside the dome. Around the spire are twelve hexagon shaped apartment complexes. We call them towers. And between the spire and the Towers lies the ring-shaped central park—the only one of its kind. That's where we're now headed."

Josh, now taking charge of the children, instructs, "Kids, form a line. I want the guest mutated children and host untainted survivor kids holding hands and watching over each other."

Whether it is by intent or otherwise, the endearing sight of the human and mutant tweens walking hand in hand around the terrarium is a terrific public relations exercise. This thought crosses Josh's mind, like it always does, as they head out in a single column with Kilia leading the front, and Josh bringing up the rear onto the astro-turfed garden.

"Simmer down, kids," Kilia restores order as the kids start to get rambunctious now that they're out in the open. A first for them all. "We've just started the tour and you'll get to play in an indoor arena in one of the towers later. We're here so I can show and tell you more."

"Let's start with Tower One, from where we just arrived. The entire basement below the counselling centre is where the inoculations and the antidote we are so dependent on are made in a sterile and detoxified environment. And directly above our level are three arenas and a convention centre. The Grand Arena which occupies half the floor has standing room for up to half a million attendees, whereas the smaller arenas and the convention centre each occupy a third of the remaining half. Arena 1 has seating and can accommodate up to 75,000 people and is usually reserved for felicitation and award functions. Arena 2, which again has standing room only, is meant for music, comedy and theatrical performances and can hold up to 150,000 people. Now, the convention centre is open to all community gatherings whether they are of ethnic, religious, or professional in nature. Even interest-based groups meet there, and that's where you will all graduate as citizens at the end of this camp."

"I never knew our home was so wonderful!" the Cooper kid exclaims, caught up in the moment.

"Yes sweetie, but listen up or you'll miss out on all the amazing facts," Kilia gently rebukes and continues at a slightly quicker pace so as not to be interrupted. "As you can see, Tower Twelve, which stands across Tower One, is the tallest with twenty stories," she points in the direction of the megalith, "while Tower One is the shortest with just two, not counting the basement of course. Notice how the heights of the towers from the first to the twelfth," Kilia keeps her flow of information going, "ascend from two stories to twenty. If you look carefully, you'll notice that the towers are hexagon shaped, just like the panes of the dome are. Each of these towers, with six sides—each 616 meters long, have an area of nearly 6 square kilometers each and are interconnected in their basements. The road you can see around this park that connects the towers on the surface level, which also links up to all the built roads in the Terrarium, is 46 meters wide. Put simply, it's an eight-lane highway."

As they enter one of the smaller towers, some of the mutated children are overjoyed by the walkalators, a sight they've never seen; while others want to run about in the serpentine corridors that have been masterfully designed so as to allow for accessibility to such a large population living in such tight spaces. Some of the residents they encounter there stop and take pictures while others look on indulgently. Untainted or otherwise, these pre-teens are a heart-warming sight.

Ensconced in the silence of one of the many elevators moving up to the level that houses a hypermarket, Kilia begins yet another outpour of information. "Alright children, listen up," she begins. "All six segments of every hexagonal floor in each Tower house a security outpost each, a supermarket, a medical centre and a maintenance depot equipped to serve the needs of the residents. Every fifth floor of all Towers has an entire segment of the hexagon dedicated to extended support facilities for healthcare, where all residents go for mandatory monthly check-ups—along with day-care, pre-primary & primary educational facilities for you children."

The elevator doors open and Josh once again organizes the group in a single file of paired up children. "Kids, now we're going to walk through a hypermarket. Look around all you want, but don't touch anything and make sure you don't disturb any of the shoppers," Josh says, giving Kilia a much-needed break from all the show and tell.

The kids silently take it all in as they walk, with some of the untainted tweens pointing at the goods they're used to seeing at home and a few exchanging whispers. As they approach the beverage section, Josh halts the column and resumes, "Alright kids, you must be a little tired and thirsty by now. You're free to sample any ready-to-serve beverage you like, carbonated or otherwise, courtesy of our Chief Administrator."

Perking up, the Cooper kid asks, "Could I have a beer?"

"You most certainly may not," Kilia replies, her consternation audible. "Not until you are of legal drinking age."

"Oh..." the Cooper kid says in mock surprise, but with a mischievous grin he adds, "I know. Dad says the same thing. I only asked because Josh said we could pick anything."

Once the beverages have been had and the sugar is starting to kick in, the children are quickly ushered to the produce section. "And now for another gift from the administration," Josh says. "Pick any one item to take back home with you."

As they proceed to the check-out counters where the empty bottles and cans are to be accounted for and disposed for recycling, and the produce picked by the children is to be processed, Jhonatan, a volunteer from Indonesia, springs to action. As they approach, he opens a closed counter and beckons them without the slightest inhibition. "Kilia, kids, step right up. Uncle Jhonatan will have you packing off, la."

After a chance meeting with her at this hypermarket once, Jhonatan had made sure he was always around when Kilia and Josh brought their young wards through. "You know we can't keep meeting like this, my lady," Jhonatan lays it on sweet and thick as he deftly swipes the selected produce by the barcode scanner and hands the items back to the kids. "How're you doing? Are those ear-rings new?"

Envying Jhonatan a little, Josh watches as the young man persists. But more, he's glad to see every ploy for attention met with stone-cold silence.

14

The Troubles and Amazing Grace

As No. 2 waits patiently in the Head of Counselling's office while she wraps up a report for the upcoming meet with the Chiefs of Staff, his eyes wander over the plethora of psychology books and journals strewn about. "And there, file saved," she says, turning to him.

"So, Head Counsellor," No. 2 inquires with a smile, "how are things?"

"Things are going reasonably well," she replies, adding, "busy, busy, busy," with a smile. "Let me give you a quick update." Picking up a sheet with tabulated figures on them, she starts off. "Of the 30 children being counselled, most seem to be coming to terms with the apocalypse, they're all more or less comfortable with the buddies they've been paired up with. They're all punctual for the sessions. They participate, and so far there have been no issues—no squabbles breaking out at the camp or at the homes they're living in. Some of the parents, the Coopers included, have opted for supplemental counselling for themselves, and I think that's helping."

"Then why the request for a meet?" the Deputy Chief Administrator asks, because everything he has heard so far sounds like music to his ears.

"If you could take a look at these," the Head of Counselling replies, placing a large stack of papers before him. "This is the artwork the children have made so far. Among other projective tests, we use these to evaluate their mental state and condition to see how well they're responding to the reality of the world they find themselves in."

There are thirty sets of five to review, but even so, No. 2 looks at them giving each its due.

Rather impressed by one set, he glances at the Head Counsellor. "Looks like we have a modern artist here."

"Those," she replies, "are done by a colour-blind child, part of her mutation."

"Oh!" No. 2 breathes, and proceeds to the next set.

Almost every child has at least one picture that features Josh or Kilia or both, and one child has even attempted to depict the entire group of pre-teens in session with their two counsellors.

One set starts out with a very well labelled drawing of Tweenland. The child who this set belongs to, clearly seems to express himself better in words because by the fifth drawing there's just shapes and adornments around what appears to be poetry. Upon closer inspection, No. 2 sees it for what it is.

He had first heard rap music at a favela street-party in Sao Paolo. And to this day he'd listen to the likes of Criolo and Emicide. Their music, his lifetime of volunteer work, he knew it all came from the same place.

Seeing him start to nod his head as he loses himself in the words and a smile on his face, the Head Counsellor interrupts softly, "I was hoping you'd look at the last set. That's why I had you look at all of the others."

"Si, si," he replies with an embarrassed grin.

The first artwork in the last set is just scrawls in black all over. The second and third feature mushroom clouds and the 'Comply' Bio-hazard Man, respectively, also in black. The fourth one features a composition of solid black and white hexagons, like the classic football pattern and the fifth is a depiction of a group of stick figures standing on one side and a solitary figure on the other.

"What do you think we can do to help this child?" No. 2 asks, gravely concerned.

"Well, I gave it quite some thought and even had a brief session with her. As it turns out, her family lives in bitter squalor even by quarantine zone standards. Her father holds down two jobs, practically working round the clock to support his large family. But they're still struggling to make ends meet."

"Will continued counselling be enough?" No. 2 asks, as repressed memories of favela children and the things they were forced to do to survive flash before his eyes.

"Not quite, she must also be given a way to take charge of the situation and realize that it won't be too long before she joins the work-force. She'll end up doing that anyway as her family won't be able to afford extended education. But she needs to be able to see the progression, each distinct step towards empowerment, not just the abstraction." No. 2 nods enthusiastically as the Head Counsellor continues. "So, can we have a Careers Day? Especially for the mutant kids, because they're likely to be influenced by this child's bleak outlook and the ways in which it manifests in the camp."

"That sounds like a great idea," No. 2 says, relief on his face. "Let me share this with the Chief Administrator today itself." As he rises from his chair, he adds, "I have much to discuss with him anyway and this will be one more action item to add to that list."

"*Hola*, Kilia, how're you today?" No. 2 inquires, bumping into her on his way out. "And how are the kids, the child staying with the Coopers, in particular?"

"Oh, she's fine, sir. Would you like to come in for a quick hello?"

Entering Tweenland, they find the children seated around Josh as he narrates his own experience from the first time he entered the terrarium and felt overwhelmed by all he saw. A little startled by the surprise visit, Josh winds up quickly and waits for Kilia to take the lead.

"Children, we have a special visitor for you today. Everyone, say hello to the Deputy Chief Administrator for the Terrarium and the greater Diablo area."

"Hello Deputy Chief Administrator," the children all greet in a sing song chorus.

"*Hola niños*, how are you all?" No. 2 responds with a broad smile. "And what did you do today?" The entire room falls silent and after a moment, Poo raises her hand tentatively.

"Yes, sweetie, why don't you tell the Deputy Chief what we did," Kilia prompts.

"We saw the Terrarium and then we went to the hypermarket and then we had a soda and then we got another present from the adminishion and then we played a lot."

As No. 2 looks at the content but exhausted children, he wonders which amongst them is the free verse poet. And which child is most in need of hope. But seeing the clock ticking on the wall, he bows out to a "Nice meeting you Deputy Chief Administrator," from the kids.

"How was your trip to the Quarantine Zone today, sir?" William asks No. 2 the moment he steps into the elevator in the spire.

"Like it always is, William."

"And Miss Paige... Did she take it well?" the young man presses, not picking up on the Deputy Chief's uncharacteristically curt response.

"It was her first time. It was no worse for her than it would have been for another."

"Well, I'm done with my action items for the day, I guess I could check in on her," William remarks, trying to play it cool. "Nice meeting you here and getting a heads up."

"That will have to wait. I think you should be present when I give the Chief Administrator my report."

"Trouble in the quarantine zone?" the Chief Administrator asks, noting the look on his deputy's face as soon as No. 2 and William are seated.

"No. Things are more or less as they should be and there was some good news on the ecological front as well, Chief, but there are other matters. I'll start off with the graffiti that's been appearing all over the quarantine zone."

"And what of it?" the Chief Administrator asks breezily. "Something we need to worry about?"

"Well, David had me meet Viktor today – a former street artist." Choosing his words carefully, No. 2 continues, "So this Viktor said it's just a bunch of kids doing something harmless, but if they're anything like him..."

William, who had so far been distracted by the thought of playing hero to a vulnerable Paige, finds himself back in the moment. Half raising his hand to get the Chief Administrator's attention, he interrupts, "Sir, if I may..."

Hearing the click from the Chief Administrator's pen, he begins, "The law of broken windows, sir. We need to nip any sign of dissent or disorder in the bud. The ideal response would be to clean up, or paint over all the graffiti as soon as it appears, irrespective of how many times it does, to drive home the message..."

"That the mutants must *comply?*" the Chief Administrator asks, cutting William off mid-sentence.

"Crafty delinquents!" William mumbles, cursing himself inwardly with far more colourful expletives.

"The only way we can deal with this is by co-opting our challengers, not confronting them out on the streets," the Chief Administrator expounds benevolently, "where it's a battle we simply cannot win." Turning to his deputy, he continues, "Speak to this Viktor person the next time you go out, No. 2, and have him arrange a meet with those responsible the time after that. Get them to soften the imagery and ideally, change 'comply' to something more harmonious. David will get them to..." the Chief Administrator pauses to revel in his choice of word, "comply."

As William looks on, his face not giving away the shocked awe he feels, No. 2 replies, "*Si*, Chief. I met with Pastor Felipe as well; his open faith church with the falafel roll business on the side is doing really well. Well enough to have saved up enough credits to commission former engineers and architects from the Quarantine Zone to draw up plans for a total makeover that includes additional housing for his staff."

"His staff?" William echoes, losing a degree of self-control.

"The ones who volunteer there for lodging and boarding," No. 2 explains quickly, and turns to his superior. "I was stunned myself, Chief, seeing the credits they've put together. He has enough to cover all costs. All he needs now is approval."

The Chief Administrator takes a moment to appreciate the chutzpah of this minister he'd heard of vaguely in the past but never really paid attention to, and gives his protégé a chance at redeeming himself. "Young William?"

"Well, it sounds like this Pastor Felipe is equating his business to some sort of a bake sale but his request for reconstruction is ludicrous," William starts off cautiously in order to get a hold of the situation before attempting an administrative judgement. "We cannot, in principle, agree because reconstruction isn't allowed in the Quarantine Zone as per charter. Furthermore, while we respect the beliefs of one and all, we can't favour any group that represents or benefits a limited number of people. Whether it be religious, cultural or social in nature, or even therapeutic in effect. Everything that generates revenue is to be treated as an enterprise and must justify the resources it consumes."

"Well done! This minister's volunteers spend their entire work-day in return for food and lodging, labour and wages. Pastor Felipe charges for a product, revenue. So..." the Chief Administer passes the verbal baton back to William who gladly takes it up with gusto.

"Pastor Felipe and his merry men will have to maintain accounts and file returns. We should start with an audit, of course. Our accountants can acquaint them with book keeping and put them on a review schedule. We must get in on the action. Not enough to bleed them dry, but just enough to keep them in check, yet profitable."

"Bravo!" the Chief Administrator beams. "William, accompany No. 2 the next time he heads out and pay Pastor Felipe a visit." Turning to his deputy, the Chief Administrator continues, "Now Jorge, if there's nothing else, we'd best head to the felicitation."

"There is a request from the Head of Counselling," No. 2 responds, rising. "But we can discuss it on our way."

⬤ #MemesFTW **Follow** • • •

So I went to the Quarantine Zone today... this isn't the best time to be writing this post, I know, but if I don't write it now, I just might end up becoming as numb as the Chief Administrator. From his memos to that UN guy, you'd think all he sees there is output, yield, targets, numbers. What a freakin' douche!

Being out there in the zone, seeing it for real, was something else. And the camp-site... I have no words. And I grew up in a trailer-park with no mother, a comatose father, a middle child.

And death rates? Wtf bro! The members of the mutant council were so chill about it. A whole lot more than I'd have been.

The journey back was even worse. There was this woman on the road, standing there with a baby in her arms, begging for credits. She said her baby's weekly antidote was overdue and anything we could spare would help.

And to think the peacekeeper would've run her over had it not been for No. 2. I just couldn't turn away and kept looking in the mirror until I couldn't see her anymore.

Luckily for me, the shit had hit the fan when I got back. Dr DeChampeaux was on the verge of decking the Head Auditor. And from the look on his face, she was already done cussing him xD

God, I just love the way she stands up for herself.

Apart from getting the Chief Administrator's schedule in line, there were a ton of his voice-memos to be transcribed as well. And I didn't have the time to think about things until William came over.

He stopped by after the Chief Administrator took off for that felicitation thing with No. 2 and asked about my visit. I guess he's a good listener because I kept going. And when I got to the part about the woman begging for her child, I was on the verge of tears.

He was trying to help, I guess, but each awkward sentence that came out of his mouth only made it worse. And then he tried to show me some lolcats on YouTube. I was like—Dude, that baby could be dead by now and you're showing me cat videos!?

Follow

He sat there quietly for a while, and then said this:

"How do you get a dead baby in a blender?

Feet first of course.

How do you get it out?

With tortilla chips..."

I was like Whaaaa? But when I saw him smile, I realized I was smiling too. And then we both had a wicked laugh as we looked up 'Dead Baby' memes. It's messed up af, I know, but I guess that's one way of dealing with a world gone to shit.

He has this really weird sense of humour but I guess he's sweet in his own way. He read my file, he stayed thru all my drama, he even made me laugh. Somebody has a thing for you, gurl...

Ok, so it just hit me. He read my file! So he must have seen my 'official' photo as well.

#BadLighting #BadHairDay #NoFilter

Aaaargghh!!!

Hmm... I think I'll bring some meatloaf for him. All I ever see him eating is cup noodles at his desk.

15

Everybody, be cool, this is a robbery

The tour of the terrarium with the kids is always the most taxing for Kilia and as she heads to the hypermarket they had been to earlier in the day, all she wants to do is finish the errand, go home and crash.

Sebastian uncle can't get enough of 'Foutou Banane' that Khady prepares and her mother affixes great importance to keeping him happy. He had been assigned to assist with their naturalization, but now he was more like family with frequent visits and marathon chat sessions with her parents that went on late into the night.

Striding through the deserted aisles, she makes her way to the exotic produce section and selects a bunch of plantains after spending a moment to pick the ones her mother would approve of. Heading to the check-out counters and seeing Jhonatan hanging around, she groans inwardly.

"Back so soon, Counsellor? I thought I'd see you again only after 3 months," he gives her the smooth treatment again as he opens up one of the unmanned stations. "Did you miss me or have you changed your mind about who you wish to spend some of your free time with? Come, let me check you out."

"Very funny, Jhonatan..." Kilia bristles. "Shouldn't your shift be over by now?"

"I'm covering for a friend, la," Jhonatan replies with a widening smile, her inflection lost on him. "I'm a good friend to have, you know. Or maybe meeting you again today was fated. What do you think?"

"I think I'm getting late," she replies, a little more brusquely than she intends to.

Jhonatan looks up from his cash register, a little crestfallen, but his expression abruptly transforms into genuine shock. "What do you want?" he asks, petrified.

It takes Kilia a moment to realize Jhonatan isn't addressing her anymore. Looking over her shoulder, she witnesses a spectacle she has never seen before.

A man in a mask, improvised from what appears to be a garment of some sort, stands holding a withered old woman hostage. He has a sharp kitchen knife at her throat and the lady, shaking like a leaf with her eyes wide, her breathing rapid, shallow and unsteady, holds steadfast to her shopping as if her life depended on it.

For a moment, the masked man doesn't answer, then in a muffled voice says, "I wa#t all the S#y7ofo@m you ha#."

"You what all the what?" Jhonatan asks genuinely as always, unable to comprehend a word.

Taking the knife off the woman's throat to cut a slit in the mask, the man screams, "STYROFOAM!!" Now crystal clear but restrained, he resumes, "Give. Me. All. The. Styrofoam. You. Have. Or. This. Woman. Dies."

His appearance out of thin air. The knife he holds to his hostage's throat in clumsy desperation. The somewhat surreal demand he has made, all leave Jhonatan puzzled but he responds with cool-headedness that even Kilia has to admire. "My friend, you can have whatever you want, just calm down and take the knife away from the lady's neck."

"I AM IN CONTROL HERE, NOT YOU, BOY!!" the masked man screams again, getting even more agitated. The lady, whose arms he's held back with his free hand, cries out in pain. "You're hurting me..."

"Don't struggle, ma'am," Jhonatan asserts. "If we co-operate, no one will get hurt. Isn't that right, sir?"

"That's right, boy!" the masked man replies, calming down just a little. "Just give me all the Styrofoam and make it quick."

"Alright then, I'll have the stock-room boys bring it from storage. We have a lot of it, packing peanuts, boards... do you have any preference?" Jhonatan asks, now starting to treat this like any other transaction.

"I WANT IT ALL, YOU IDIOT!!" the masked man starts screaming again. "Tell them to bring it here, in garbage bags. Tell them to load it on three carts!"

Jhonatan relays the instructions over the P.A. system as calmly as he can and they wait as second after painful second ticks by.

After the stock-room boys leave the laden carts by the check-out counter, the masked man instructs, "Alright, now I want you," as he points directly at Jhonatan, "pushing the first cart out to the garbage disposal in the stairwell closest to this hypermarket. The second cart will be pushed by this old lady and the third cart, I want a woman pushing. You," he says, pointing at Kilia, "you will push the cart behind me."

Once they get there, the masked man continues, "Drop the bags down the chutes," taking the old lady aside, knife still at her throat. His mask, now soaked with perspiration, clings to his face making him look even more ominous.

"You and the girl can go." The man in the mask says. "The lady stays," once all the bags are despatched.

"But we did all you wanted..." Kilia starts to protest weakly.

"JUST GO!"

As the door closes behind Jhonatan and Kilia, the masked man bounds down the stairs, leaving the lady petrified but otherwise unharmed. Unsure of what to do next, she stumbles back to the hypermarket where the floor supervisor has Jhonatan and Kilia waiting for the peacekeepers. Seeing the old lady approach, Jhonatan turns to her, "Ma'am, are you alright? Let's get you inside so you can sit down, have a drink of water..."

Soon enough, two peacekeepers burst into the hypermarket and are pointed in the direction of the break room where Kilia, Jhonatan and the old lady are recuperating. The peacekeepers, after getting the gist of the incident, seem baffled. Not only by the spoils the masked man was after but the crime as well because not only was a stick-up unprecedented, they don't even have protocols or guidelines to follow as standard operating procedure.

"Mrs Katzoff, I'm sorry I have to ask this of you," one of the peacekeeper says, "but we need to file a report. So, could you—all three of you, come with us?"

"Don't worry, ma'am, it'll all be over soon," Kilia comforts the fragile old lady, one arm around her shoulder for support, as they walk to the security outpost. The lady, shaken by her ordeal, keeps rambling about her groceries and that awful man while the peacekeepers applaud Jhonatan's handling of the situation.

The peacekeepers attempt to contact the Chief of Security but end up speaking to his deputy.

"Despatch a team to the garbage dumpsters immediately," the Deputy Chief of Security directs his shift supervisor.

"Scour the basement for any sign of activity. Question any witnesses they come across. There are no cameras down there; we'll have to rely on human-intel."

The gravity of the situation isn't lost on the Deputy Chief of Security as he paces the command centre in the administrative office. "If only they had the decency to smuggle discreetly like the Krokodil supply chain does," he mutters under his breath.

Soon enough a video call comes through. "Sir, the dumpsters were empty by the time we got here. They timed it well. The Styrofoam must be on its way out in a garbage truck," the peacekeeper on-screen reports.

"Return to your post," the Deputy Chief of Security instructs, ending the transmission and continues pacing.

"Lockdown, sir?" the shift-supervisor manning the central control console asks.

"We could lock the Terrarium down, but that'll cause panic," the Deputy Chief of Security replies, thinking out loud more than making a decision. After a moment of thought, he relays the order. "Let the trucks through, it's just Styrofoam. We should be focussing on the perpetrator. Pull up footage from cameras at all elevator bays on all levels, starting from when the hostages were released and scan for any suspicious activity."

Stepping out of the security outpost after having their statements recorded, Jhonatan turns to Kilia. "Shall we first escort Mrs Katzoff to her quarters after which I can drop you to yours?"

"I'll be fine," Kilia replies. "But Mrs Katzoff could use some support. Thank you Jhonatan."

Plantains in hand, Kilia makes her way home, shaken to the core. Stepping in, she finds Tidjane watching cartoons on the entertainment unit. "What took you so long?" Khady begins, but noticing the pallid look on her daughter's face, falls silent.

16

Crewmen. Crooning.

Striking a jaunty pose, with his trademark sunglasses on, Bono stands on stage in Arena 1 singing 'Radioactive'. An ardent supporter of human rights and front-man for U2, the living legend has the construction workers of Eden (925) in rapture.

Radioactive, the 'Imagine Dragons' hit which had been released barely two months before the apocalypse, by the sheer dint of its timing was considered prophetic by some, politically incorrect by many, and a little insensitive by most. Everyone in the audience, however, seems to be having a blast with quite a few even joining in on the chorus.

"We love you, Diablo!!!" Bono's voice reverberates over the ebbing cheers, concluding the first set for the evening. "We're going to take a break now, but we'll be back to rock you some more once the speeches have been made and the awards handed out. Thank you!!"

The Chief of Engineering walks out from one of the wings and meets Bono about halfway between the centre and the podium. Thanking Bono, he takes the microphone and turns to the audience. "Give it up for U2, everyone! Had they not stopped by on their 'World Terrarium Tour', it would've just been me and those little babies over there," he says, pointing at the stage hands carrying in a table with commemorative plaques on it. As the band walks off the stage, the audience breaks into an energetic ovation with some even jumping to their feet.

Glancing over his shoulder to ensure the set up for the Chief Administrator and his deputy are in order, the Chief of Engineering continues as the house lights are dimmed. "But seriously, we've done well in the six months that have gone by and if we don't deserve this night, I don't know who does. To do the honours, I give you our very own... Chief Administrator!!"

Stepping into the spotlight that tracks them, the Chief Administrator strides purposefully to the podium set up at the centre, followed by No. 2.

"How many men does it take to screw in a light-bulb," the Chief Administrator begins the moment the glare is on him, his voice soft and controlled, his hands clasped behind his back and his pen held at the ready, his lapel-mike tested and in place. The raucous audience straining to hear him quietens down immediately and he resumes only when he hears his pen clicking at two-second intervals.

"We've all heard variations of that old joke," the Chief Administrator whispers into the microphone, and then asks just a little more audibly. "But I ask you, how many construction workers does it take to build a Terrarium?"

He waits, and after a moment, turns to the audience in the near left. "Anyone here care to hazard a guess?" His question punctuated by the pen in his hand, pointing at the section he has tendered the question to. After waiting long enough for the silence to get oppressive, he turns abruptly to the audience at the far right, pen pointed in his hand fully extended and repeats his question in an even firmer tone, "Anyone?"

Standing there, alone in the spotlight, he feels his audience squirm under his merciless baton.

"The answer, my fellow mutated humans, untainted survivors," he lets them off the hook, clasping his hands behind his back once again, "is all of them. It's going to take each and every one of you to build our terrarium. And the rate at which we're going, we're going to get there perhaps even a year ahead of schedule. So, give yourselves a big hand!"

As his words elicit deafening applause, the Chief Administrator smiles inwardly, knowing all too well that his audience's joy is overpowered by relief.

Waiting long enough for the clicks of his pen to become audible to him once again, he steps away from the podium and begins walking the length of the stage. With both the spotlight on him and his wireless microphone allowing him to feign rumination, he continues, "When President Kennedy was visiting the NASA space centre, he asked a man carrying a broom—a janitor, I imagine—so he asked this man what he did there. And to his credit, the man replied, Mr President, I'm helping put a man on the moon."

Pausing just long enough to let that sink in, the Chief Administrator continues, "In the immutable words of Adrienne Clarkson, *Each of us is carving a stone, erecting a column, or cutting a piece of glass in the construction of something much bigger than ourselves.*"

A voice from the back cries "Hear, hear" and cheers erupt across the gathering.

"You, my fellow volunteers and the people of Diablo valley," with his pen-bearing hand at the ready, "You aren't just digging holes and pouring concrete," he raises his pen as if clutching a battle-flag. "You are building Eden!!" The words aren't lost on a single construction worker present and the arena begins rumbling towards a crescendo. "We are here, all of us, to take the work done by those who came in before us forward." Now speaking over the applause in a commanding voice, "and leave something for those who come in after we are long gone to build on. In the years to come, if we keep marching forward at this pace, the foundations for the homes in the areas outside the apartment tower grid will be laid and those of you who plan on continuing the job you've had here, in other, newer terrariums, will carry on; leaving behind those who intend to make Eden (925) their home and continue taking the work here to the next stage."

The sobering thought coupled with the change in the Chief Administrator's body language has its intended effect.

"So how did we get here ahead of schedule, with a remarkable lead on our counterparts at terrariums across the world? I don't have to tell you about the hours you've put in, the sweat you've wiped from your brows, the tremendous discipline and consistency you've displayed but what I want to say, I believe President Kennedy said best and I quote, *All this will not be finished in the first one hundred days. Nor will it be finished in the first one thousand days, nor in the life of this Administration. But let us begin. In your hands, my fellow citizens, more than mine, will rest the final success or failure of our course."*

As he mouths the words of a true believer with all the sincerity he can muster and waits for the cheering to subside, the Chief Administrator's thoughts turn to Winston Churchill's 'Finest Hour' speech. He had decided, at the last minute, to drop that and use JFK's inaugural address instead for the sake of continuity and to appease the mutants, of course.

"So without further ado, let us honour those who have distinguished themselves at one of the hardest jobs the administration could assign, the one most essential for all mankind... reconstruction!"

He nods at the Chief of Engineering who begins calling out the names and titles of the award recipients one by one and waits for them to reach the stage where he shakes hands with them while No. 2 hands out a commemorative plaque and citation.

The last and most coveted award at the ceremony is for the 'Crewman of the Year'. The selection criterion for this one are the toughest and exhaustive all-round appraisals are carried out since every one of the thousands of construction workers present is eligible. The Chief of Engineering is the only one to know who has won and this well-guarded secret adds an air of mystery to the entire ceremony.

"And finally, the Crewman of the year," the Chief of Engineering announces from the wings. "This year's winner is... Sebastian Callaghan!"

As the whole arena erupts in applause, Sebastian makes his way to the stage in a daze. After shaking hands with the Chief Administrator, collecting his plaque and citation from No. 2, he asks to thank his crew. The Chief Administrator hands him his lapel microphone with an approving smile.

"Thank you... for this unexpected honour," Sebastian begins, a little overwhelmed. "I just want to thank my crew for the outstanding work they've put in. Could you all stand up, lads, and take a bow?" As they rise from their seats, Mr Sebastian thanks each and every one by name, saving his favourite for last. "And Josh," he concludes. "Even though he works half a day, he does more than the work of two men. Keep it up laddie!"

With the last award having been given out, the Chief Administrator and No. 2 make their way back to their seats as the band strides onto the stage amidst cheers and woo-hoos from the audience.

As Bono kicks off the second set on an apt and resonant note, the Chief Administrator makes an inconspicuous exit leaving his deputy to be his face for the rest of the show. His eyes and ears as well.

Stopping on his way out at one of the restrooms by the exit, glad to find it deserted, the Chief Administrator whistles one of the tunes he's heard as he relieves himself.

Making his way out of the arena, he bumps into Sebastian.

"Leaving early, sir?"

"Yes, long day," the Chief Administrator replies with a plastic smile.

"Well, sir," Sebastian begins as they descend the stairs to the ground level. "While I have your attention today, and this opportunity, could we have a word?"

"I prefer tending to official matters in office, Mr Callaghan, is it?"

"Yes, sir, but I've made several applications for consideration," Sebastian presses, "but they all come back with a big red rejected stamped on them."

"Alright," the Chief Administrator acquiesces. "I'll make an exception for the Crewman of the year. Go on."

"Well, sir," Sebastian begins haltingly. "This is about Josh, one of my crew. He's had a hard life and even now, he sleeps on the streets in the Quarantine Zone..."

"He works in construction," the Chief Administrator interrupts, "surely he can afford better."

"Aye, but he's given up his quarters for a senior citizen he supports. He's a good lad, hard worker, never gave me a reason to complain..."

"So you want to pay him more than the UN standard? I'm afraid that's not possible," the Chief Administrator says, cutting Mr Sebastian off.

"No, sir, I was hoping he could stay inside for the six working days. That way he'd have access to facilities and..."

"That is simply out of the question," the Chief Administrator interrupts emphatically, stopping Sebastian dead in his tracks. "No wonder all your applications were rejected. But tell you what, if you're in need of companionship of any sort, don't hesitate to reach out. I'm sure we can arrange something to suit your taste. Be sure to write to my Deputy directly. And keep up the good work!"

Horrified at having been misconstrued to this extent, "Thank you, sir," is all Sebastian can manage.

By the time the Chief Administrator reaches his apartment in Tower Twelve, he finds an urgent message awaiting him.

"There's been a situation, Chief Administrator," the Chief of Security says in the recording. "Please call me back, sir, no matter what time it is."

"Yes, Captain, the situation?" the Chief Administrator asks the moment his call is answered.

"Well, sir, a hypermarket was held-up earlier today. The perpetrator wanted all the Styrofoam they had and made off with it. He took a hostage as well."

"Anyone injured?" the Chief Administrator inquires.

"No, sir."

"Any leads?"

"My deputy's still scanning the CCTV footage from all elevator bays in the Tower," the Chief of Security answers. "But the assailant most likely disappeared through the basements."

"And what of the Styrofoam?"

"Unfortunately, sir, I was conducting an advanced hand to hand combat course at the time and my deputy didn't order an immediate lockdown. I take full responsibility, but the Styrofoam went out with the rest of the garbage."

"Suggestions to avoid such instances in the future?" the Chief Administrator asks.

"All stairwells be fitted with motion sensor activated cameras, basements too."

"But why Styrofoam?"

"We've been asking ourselves the same question. I guess my deputy was justified in not going to Def-Con. Styrofoam has no value, can do no real damage."

"Yes, no real damage," the Chief Administrator echoes, hoping this doesn't snowball into something bigger. "Alright, Captain, thank you for this timely report. Please submit one in writing to my office tomorrow so we can requisition the resources to do the needful. Good night."

76 DAYS AGO: ANOTHER DAY OF REST

17

Being Goth. Doing Drugs.
& the Imperative

As he stands waiting for the familiar voice, Josh is taken aback when the door is answered by an attractive Asian mutant dressed in punk goth. "You must be Josh," she says, as he wonders if he's knocked on the wrong door.

"I'm Aiko," she purrs. "Dr Hudson talks about you all the time. He even said you'd be here soon, come on in," leaving the door ajar, she strides back in with feline grace. "I'll introduce you to Viktor."

Following her inside, Josh sees Viktor lounging on his chair as Aiko curls up on Viktor's lap without the slightest inhibition saying, "Viktor, meet Josh. The benefactor."

"Josh the benefactor," Viktor says with a smirk. "While Doctor is in restroom, let us know each other."

Uncomfortable with the situation he finds himself in, Josh remains standing fixed to his spot, torn between his instinct to look away and his utter and absolute inability to do so.

"Sit down Josh, relax," Aiko says cattily. "This is your home, after all."

Wordlessly placing the sack of supplies he's carrying next to the empty chair that the Doctor always sits on, Josh settles down. "And won't you tell us about yourself?" Aiko prods. "Because all we hear from Dr Hudson is how wonderful you are and how you spend everything you make in order to keep him going *etcetera et al.*"

"We actually very grateful for that," Viktor interjects, in a surprisingly appreciative, even if rough tone.

"I do what I can," Josh responds, forcing a smile.

"And you do... what?" Aiko persists.

"I work in construction. In the Terrarium, and I counsel mutated and untainted children as well," Josh replies quietly. Anxiously awaiting the good doctor's return. "Help them come to terms with the apocalypse," he struggles with sentence formation, "form bonds with one another, share the vision for humanity, you know..."

"So you brainwash children for UN in morning. And build their homes in evening. How noble," Viktor remarks, his voice laced with sarcasm.

"It pays the bills," Josh counters, his eyes aflame.

"Evil can only take hold of consenting soul," Viktor comments in his tone of practiced disinterest. Pleased with himself, however, to get a rise out of Josh. And even more pleased to quote an author who made him the man he was, Viktor plants the seeds of doubt in a young man who might someday be turned. "Ursula Leguin, a great American novelist say quite a bit on that. Maybe you find her work in your private library. Many great minds like her, they say, for us to imagine a world without capitalism, we have to first imagine apocalypse and dystopia. That was my time. That happen already, and you still build bars of own cage?"

"Viktor..." Aiko interrupts softly, salaciously tracing the serpentine tattoo on his neck, "He's one of the counsellors at Tweenland." Turning back to Josh, she continues, "Working with kids all year round... That's so adorable! Are you on the bus that comes out with the untainted children to drop the mutant kids off?"

A little disturbed by the extent of knowledge this brazen couple seem to have of his work, his basement and books, all Josh can manage is a forced nod.

Just then, Dr Hudson steps in the room. "Doctor, Josh has arrived," Aiko purrs.

As he rises from the chair the Doctor usually occupies, Josh notices a subtle shift in Viktor's posture and attitude. "Would you give me a moment? There's something I need to wrap up with these two," Dr Hudson says. "So Viktor, you were saying the goods have arrived..."

"Yes, Doctor," Viktor replies, his voice tinged with humility. "Soup will be bottled and ready in time, team have already been rehearsing play."

"Good, good," the doctor nods in approval. "And now that Josh is here..."

"Yes, doctor. We go." Viktor says, rising with Aiko.

Aiko hugs Dr Hudson and whispers something that's too soft for Josh's ears while Viktor waits to shake hands with Dr Hudson. And he does, with a slight bow. Seeing the bow register in Josh's eyes, Aiko turns to Josh and flashes him an impish smile.

"Don't they make a good couple?" Dr Hudson remarks, turning to Josh with a look of contentment on his face as the door closes behind them. "There's that bit of an age difference but aren't they bliss personified, just the same?"

Josh feels a little unsettled from the whole experience and meekly takes his place in his usual chair.

"You know, son, you should stop bothering about this withered old man, find someone and move in here. I've outlived my usefulness and now believe I've done all that can be, for our cause, as well."

WHO WAS HE? I'VE NEVER SEEN HIM HERE BEFORE.
OH, HE'S A GOLD DIGGER. I HEAR HE MAKES AND SELLS KROKODIL ON THE SIDE.
YOU KNOW, THE DRUG THE RUSSIANS MADE BACK IN THE DAY. THE ONE THAT DEFORMS THE SKIN OF USERS GIVING IT A CROCODILE-LIKE APPEARANCE.
I KNOW WHAT KROKODIL IS, DOC. EVERYONE IN THE QUARANTINE ZONE DOES. AND I KNOW ENOUGH TO STAY AS FAR AWAY FROM IT AS I CAN. WHY DO YOU ASSOCIATE WITH SUCH A PERSON?
YOU DISLIKE HIM BECAUSE OF WHAT HE DOES?
WHAT HE DOES FOR A LIVING MAKES HIM WHO HE IS, DOES IT NOT?
AH, THE BEING VERSUS DOING CONUNDRUM.. HE DOES WHAT HE DOES IN ORDER TO SURVIVE.
WELL, HE CERTAINLY LOOKS LIKE A SURVIVOR!!
WE'VE BEEN DISCUSSING PHILOSOPHY FOR A WHILE. LET'S EXAMINE VIKTOR'S DOING WITH HIS BEING IN THAT LIGHT.
SOCRATES SAID - TO BE IS TO DO; SARTRE - TO DO IS TO BE; AND SINATRA - DO, BE, DO, BE, DO.. DO, DO, DEE, DA.. LA, DI, DA, DI, DAIYAA.. RA, RA, RA.. RA.. AND SO ON...

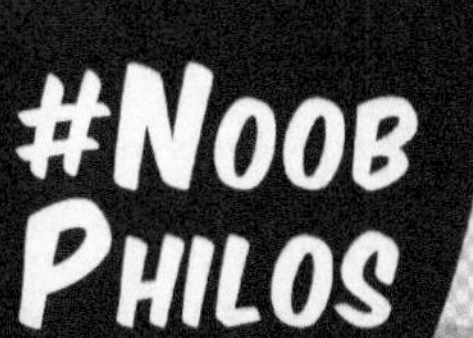

#NOOB PHILOS

SOCRATES WAS AN ANCIENT GREEK PHILOSOPHER, VERY INFLUENTIAL ON THE WESTERN SCHOOL. THE 'ALLEGORY OF THE CAVE' IS ONE OF PLATO'S WIDELY KNOWN SOCRATIC DIALOGUES. WE SPOKE OF THAT.
SARTRE WAS A KEY FIGURE IN THE PHILOSOPHY OF EXISTENTIALISM, YOU REMEMBER OUR DISCUSSION ON GODOT, YES?
AND FRANK SINATRA, PART OF THE ORIGINAL RAT PACK, A MAN AFTER MY OWN HEART... ONE OF HIS SONGS, 'STRANGERS IN THE NIGHT' ENDED ON HIM SCATTING THE BIT I JUST DID... BUT YOU WOULDN'T HAVE HEARD IT.
A SONG, DOC... REALLY?
JOSHIE, I'M NOT SURE WHO PUT THE THREE STATEMENTS TOGETHER. BUT ITS ORIGIN MAY BE TRACED TO ANOTHER STREET-ARTIST.
...
ALRIGHT THEN.. PICTURE THIS: WE MUTANTS FIND OURSELVES IN A RATHER PRECARIOUS POSITION. WHEN HOW LONG WE'LL BE ABLE TO SURVIVE THE ANTHROPOCENE, OR RATHER, FOR HOW LONG WE'LL BE ABLE TO KEEP GOING TO THAT SO-CALLED HOSPITAL AND GET THAT DAMN ANTIDOTE IS IN QUESTION, KROKODIL OFFERS A BRIEF RESPITE..

"Some have even reported positive side effects, not unlike the ones marijuana affords cancer patients. You must take that into account before you decide what is or isn't acceptable."

"Hmm... so, the play Viktor was talking about?" Josh asks after a moment of reflection. "Play as in theatre, right?"

"I don't want to spoil it for you but I promise you'll get to see it from the front row," the doctor replies and veers the conversation back. "In the final analysis, it isn't what Viktor does in his spare time that makes him good or bad, but simply who he is. In the morally relativistic realm of Time Structuring, at least."

"Time Structuring?" Josh asks reluctantly, sensing a new topic coming on, one he would've been glad to learn about on any other day but this one.

"It's quite simple really. We have X amount of time on the planet, the sum total of all the time that makes up what we call our life. And Y is the amount of time we spend doing what we must do in order to survive. X, the time we have, minus Y, the time we lose in order to stay alive leaves out Z. Z, the time we have to spend as we please. Going back to being and doing - where we got started. What we do with Z is that which makes us be. And being who we are, dictates what we end up doing with Z. The labels we mistakenly attribute to ourselves come from Y."

"Doc, sorry, but I'm getting a little lost here."

"Viktor harvests transmuted metal for eight hours a day, six days a week. This makes him a gold-digger: the label from Y."

"And he deals Krokodil on the side," Josh adds, getting snarky.

"Of course," Dr Hudson admits freely. But that's him spending his free time, Z—time that he could've spent doing something fun with Aiko, for instance. We know he has money to burn from all the gold. But he chooses to spend it helping fellow mutants deal with their pain. Do you not see nobility in that? Even if in savage form, if you must?"

His regret over the tone he just took and the realization that the Doctor's mind was already made-up, keeps Josh from saying more.

"The way I see it," Dr Hudson continues, mistaking Josh's silence for agreement, "those at the top of the time food-chain are the ones who help us structure our spare time, the Z element of ourselves. And in doing so, they give us meaning and purpose. Whether they are family members—who make us caring parents, husbands, wives, daughters or sons. Or celebrities and their frequent relationship status updates, their wardrobe malfunctions—who make us adoring fans or journalists. Even this conversation we are having, makes us suspect. As our time here is being structured by philosophers from a bygone era, who, as I've said before, ask questions we wouldn't even think to articulate, and sometimes provide thought provoking answers as well. But the self-anointed philosophers of today, though, deludedly immersing themselves in the pursuit of questions made long redundant, insisting upon building on them—those are the bane of my existence.

"The what of your what?" Josh asks, so at sea, he fumbles at the turn of the phrase.

"My problem with philosophy, I mean."

As his pupils dilate to normalcy, Josh wonders whether his mentor had been shooting up some Krokodil when he arrived earlier as the good doctor rambles on.

"Once upon a time, philosophers were the thinkers, the rationalists, the scientists. They created the constructs we built our wisdom on but as mankind's collective body of knowledge increased, silos began to form. Philosophy became so abstract and self-referential, it ultimately lost touch with the actual reality we live in. Remember Zeno? Are we to entertain his paradox of the arrow? An arrow in motion when considered at any instant is stationary. Therefore, as Zeno would have it, it isn't moving at all. But the truth is, there is no time to measure since we are considering only an instant. In any instant, there can be no speed. Given that speed is a function of distance over time. While the philosophical bow ties itself up neatly, the consideration of a fraction when excluding the divisor is not only irrational, it's rationally irreprehensible."

Josh, glad to have the good doctor back, replies with a laugh, "You don't have to get so technical, Doc. You had me convinced the last time when you had said, 'If you really want to know if the arrow let loose by the man at point A is stationary, ask the man at point B with the bull's-eye painted on his back'. And it's not like being rational has anything to do with square roots and negative numbers. Or the ratio of the circumference of a circle to its diameter."

"FLATLAND!" Both the master and the disciple scream in unison.

"And I'm sure you recall our discussion on the Myth of Sisyphus, a phenomenal piece of literature, comparable to Godot even," the Doctor continues excitedly. "But when Sisyphus invents a machine that rolls the rock up the mountain for him, what then?"

Pausing to catch his breath, he starts off feverishly, "As for Baudrillard, still bogging us down with the story of the map and the territory as the precursor to his thesis, I have but three words—Try. Google. Earth. Call it an agenda, if you must."

Breaking off into cackles that finally calm him down, the Doctor concludes, "Wittgenstein had some very interesting propositions. Senseless, as he himself called them. But suffice it to say, philosophy must be subject to the rigorous light of reason we hold religions, or isms of any sort, up to."

Seeing the light extinguished from Josh's eyes, Dr Hudson leans over and comforts the closest thing to a son he has. "Do what you would have anyone do for everyone. At all times. *That* is the Categorical Imperative. That is all you need to know."

"Protect yourself from pain as you must, son, but never be afraid to die for a just cause."

18

A Game of Traditions

"That must be Sebastian uncle, I'll get it!" Tidjane screams excitedly, bounding towards the door.

Alasco follows him with just as much anticipation, and after Sebastian has handed Tidjane a present wrapped in brown paper and ruffled his hair a little, he hugs the man he feels closest to in the terrarium. "Sebastian... *i ni chè.*"

"Kilia!" Khady calls out. "Brother Sebastian is here. Put that iPad away and join us." Turning to Sebastian, she adds, "Kilia's on that thing all the time. If she could find a way to talk to us through that, she'd probably tell us more," and modestly embraces him.

"Mom, can I open the present now or do I have to wait until later?" Tidjane asks but before Khady can answer, Alasco cuts in, "No, no, there's no need to wait. It's a special present, a game. And we're all going to play."

Hearing this, Tidjane forgets all his lessons on recycling and rips through the brown paper. Opening the box and seeing its contents, he looks up despondently. "It's just a piece of wood and a bunch of stones."

Sebastian beams with amusement and both Alasco and Khady look upon Tidjane with indulgent smiles. Still confused, Tidjane takes a closer look and asks, "Am I supposed to toss the stones into the pits from a distance?"

"No, Djane," Alasco replies. "It's an Oware set. It's made from wood. A very precious commodity. And the stones are made from concrete. Uncle Sebastian made us a game set that we grew up playing back home in Mali. A game set you can't buy but one you have to make with your own hands. He made it especially so that we could all share our culture."

"Don't forget to thank Sebastian uncle for it," Khady adds. "He hand-crafted it for us."

"Thank you, uncle!" Tidjane says, his excitement returning. "Can we play now?"

"Hello, uncle!" Kilia exclaims, finally making an appearance. "How are you?"

"I'm fine, Kilia. It's good to see ya; and how is work?" The conversation is very guarded while Tidjane is around to keep the Santa Claus version of his world intact.

"Sit, brother, sit while I go get us something to drink," Khady says. "Beer as always, right?" she confirms before heading to the kitchen. "Aye, a pint is good," Sebastian replies with a smile, taking a seat on the couch.

Settling next to him, Alasco eagerly awaits the beer he drinks only when Sebastian visits. He knows he shouldn't be drinking at all, since intoxication is forbidden by his faith, but his love for a brother has softened his heart.

"So uncle, how are your sons doing?" Kilia asks, from across the coffee table.

"Oh, they're fine. Their families as well. This distance between Ireland and Diablo is doing us good."

Barely has Khady returned with the beers that Tidjane begins, "Can we play now?"

"Djane," Alasco rebukes. "Sebastian Uncle is going to be here all evening, there's no rush," uncapping the bottles, Alasco and Sebastian clink them in unison with a *"Sláinte!"*

"So, brother Sebastian," Khady gets the conversation going as Alasco and Sebastian have their first swig, savouring the taste of the brew, "Alasco was telling me you're doing well at work."

"Aye, all construction projects are doing well. Most crews are running optimally and we're beating our targets."

"Stop being so modest, brother," Alasco interjects. "Tell Khady about the award you won."

Smiling self-effacingly, Sebastian adds, "Aye, so I got this award, from the big man himself."

"Crewman of the year!" Alasco exclaims. "The awards committee chose him from the construction workers, supervisors and managers, all put together. That calls for a celebration my friend. *Sláinte!*" Reaching out, he clinks Sebastian's bottle a second time.

"Can we play the game now?" Tidjane pipes up once again.

Seeing the irritation build up on Alasco's face, Sebastian intervenes, "Sure Djane, even I'm curious about how it works." Turning to Alasco, he says, "You'll teach us, won't you?"

"Alright, but let me tell you a little story first," Alasco starts off. "It's a legend of the Asante people. There was a man and a woman and they began playing this game. As they played, they began falling in love. And as they kept playing, their love for each other and the game grew. They didn't want to stop and they didn't want to play with anyone else either. The village elders got them married so that they could play happily ever after. That's where the name comes from.

'Oware' in Twi, the language of the Asante people, means 'they married'."

"Enough with the legends, father," Kilia says, a wide smile on her face. "Tell them how to play the game already, or I will."

"Alright, alright; you young people are so impatient! So, the objective of the game is to end up with as many of the seeds as possible."

"Seeds?" Tidjane asks.

"The stones are the seeds, son, and the wooden board is the field. When the game starts off, all the seeds are evenly distributed on both sides of the board. Four seeds in each of the six small pits facing one another. The two larger pits are where the harvested seeds go, the large pit on the right-hand side belongs to each player—see, one for each player," Alasco says, pointing at the board as he explains. "Now let's play one game so I can explain as we go along. Djane, Sebastian, why don't the two of you play, since you are both new to this."

After the board is set up, Alasco continues with the instructions. "Now the two of you take turns to move your seeds from one pit to another. When you move the seeds, you deposit them one by one in the other pits in a counter clockwise direction. And since this is the first time, we'll play with the simpler rules. So as you move your seeds, you also get to place them in the harvest pit on your right. The idea is to capture all the seeds you can into that one because all the seeds that end up in your harvest pit are yours and cannot be captured by your opponent. Just one last thing to remember, when you place a seed in a pit that has no seeds, you capture that one seed and all the seeds in the corresponding pit on your opponent's side as well. Shall we start with our first game now?"

"Sounds simple enough to me," Sebastian responds. "What do you say, Djane, shall we begin?"

"Yes, uncle!" Tidjane exclaims. Turning to his mother, he adds, "But ma, you've gotta help me."

"Right after I get some more beer," Khady replies, heading for the kitchen again.

The game begins and both Tidjane and Sebastian end up making classic beginner mistakes. Tidjane counts his moves out loud and plays cautiously while Sebastian, starting to feel light headed, plays without a care. The game ends rather quickly and neither Sebastian nor Tidjane understand how Sebastian ended up winning.

"Let's play again, uncle, and ma, you've got to help me this time," Tidjane insists.

"But that's not fair, Djane," Sebastian laughs. "I'm as new to this as you are. Maybe your father can help me, right Alasco?"

"Alright, but I haven't played for ages, and Khady has always been better. But why not!"

They set up the board for a rematch and this time, the game goes on for a lot longer as Khady and Alasco end up taking over on Tidjane and Sebastian's behalf. Alasco, a little voluble now that he's two beers down, explains each move that's being made as he guides Sebastian's hand. Khady, getting competitive, has her brows furrowed with a sharp focus on the board, saying nothing as she points at the pit from which she wants Tidjane to move the seeds.

The game eventually comes to an end with Khady winning. And Tidjane starts hopping up and down in a little victory dance, singing, "Ole, ole, ole, ole. Ole... ole..."

"Kilia, could you take Djane to your room and play?" Khady says. "So us grown-ups can talk? So, brother, did you hear anything about the robbery?" Khady asks, as soon as she's sure Tidjane is out of earshot.

"Khady..." Alasco says reproachfully. "We don't know that for sure. The news bulletin only mentioned it as 'The Styrofoam Incident'."

"Come now, Alasco..." Khady retorts. "Kilia was there. Remember what she said about the old lady being held at knifepoint?" Turning to Sebastian, she continues with her inquisition, "Do you think the outsiders were involved?"

"Outsiders?" Sebastian asks, not understanding the euphemism.

"The mutants, Sebastian..." Alasco clarifies in a whisper. "We refer to them as outsiders because we dare not use the 'M' word around Djane."

"Or was it someone from the inside with criminal tendencies?" Khady demands, turning to Alasco. "Like that gang-member from your African social." Aware immediately, of having shown disrespect to her husband in public, Khady cocks her head to one side and mutters, "I can't believe I still let you take Djane to those things."

Just then, Tidjane steps in and Khady, Alasco and Sebastian freeze. But the child appears not to have noticed anything, and taking a bag of chips from the kitchen, heads back inside.

"Well, Khady, from what little I've heard," Sebastian says, "I don't think the, ahem, outsiders were involved, but then again, it's too early to be able to say for sure, since the contraband hasn't been traced."

Sebastian's intonation isn't lost on Alasco, who, laughing nervously, says, "You must think we're very tribal, brother... But you know..."

Sebastian raises his hands as he replies, "I understand. I'm getting touchy in my old age is all." He lowers his gaze and adds dejectedly, "Because they won't let me bring Josh in."

"Josh?" Alasco asks. "That boy Kilia works with? When they'd just started, all she'd talk about was him. Khady even had to sit her down and explain..."

"That's when she started spending more and more time with her iPad, right Alasco?" Khady adds, acrimoniously. And turning to Sebastian, she continues, "But what were you saying about Josh, brother?" Khady asks. "You wanted to bring him in? You mean inside?"

"Yes," Sebastian sighs. "Just trying to help the lad is all. He could have roomed in the shanty at our construction site but the administration just won't consider my request."

What is it about this outsider and the effect he has on the people, Alasco wonders as Khady excuses herself to heat the Poulet Yassa and Foutou Banane.

19

An Incendiary Ingredient

The Chief Administrator lounges on his couch watching his favourite sitcom. He's watched all seasons of 30 Rock before, but he now watches the show, one episode at a time, right before going to bed. He had spent most of the day with David.

Getting a sense of the mood in the Quarantine Zone, reviewing the motion graphics that would accompany his 'fire-side chat' addresses to the mutant populace and brain-storming the first script. His public speaking methodology was limited to Googling opening jokes and end-quotes but David took things to a whole new level. *It's good to have discovered Davie,* he thinks to himself. But the game of squash they'd played, and he lost, had worn him out as well and he finds himself yawning.

'Sun-Tea,' the sixth episode of the fourth season of 30 Rock is at a particularly delightful moment when the Chief Administrator receives an incoming video call. Smiling inwardly at the punchline that was interrupted, the Chief Administrator switches to communication mode on the console. And an unsettled looking Dr DeChampeaux, his Chief of Science, in wrinkled bed-clothes fills the screen. "Bon soir, chérie. And to what do I owe the pleasure of this call?" he inquires.

The sarcasm isn't lost on her as she begins in her heavily accented voice. "Chief Administrator, I am sorry to bother you so late but I overheard a conversation yesterday. One of my junior scientists was joking about how he'd read a recipe for making napalm in his student days when he was dating an armchair anarchist."

"And...?"

"Styrofoam can be mixed with gasoline to make napalm."

"WHAT?"

"Yes, as long as you get the proportions right, you can make Grade-A Napalm." Dr DeChampeaux continues, "All you have to do is mix it, *et voila, c'est fin.*"

"And you're telling me this now?!"

"*Je suis désolé*, Chief Administrator! They were joking... I didn't pay attention, but earlier today it came back to me and I've been restless ever since. I thought I'd disturb you even though it is so late."

"You did the right thing, Dr DeChampeaux, sooner would have been better but even so," the Chief Administrator says, now wide awake. "If you'll excuse me, I have a few calls of my own to make." Ending the call abruptly, he taps the contacts section on the universal remote, scrolls down to the Chief of Security's number and connects.

The Chief of Security's wife is on the screen moments later and seeing him, says politely, "I'll get my husband, sir, he's in the other room." Soon enough, the Chief of Security appears on the display, his game-face on, "Yes, Chief Administrator?"

"You remember the conversation we first had about the stolen Styrofoam and the purpose it might serve?" the Chief Administrator asks.

"Yes, sir. Styrofoam is used for packing and shipping, not much else. We put the case on the back burner."

"Here's another answer," the Chief Administrator snaps back. "It can also be used to make napalm!"

"I should have thought of that!" the Chief of Security explodes, furious with himself. "On all my rotations, we dealt with IEDs and suicide bombers only. Napalm wasn't the weapon of choice for those Camel-Jock..." But stopping himself before finishing the slur, he asks, "How should we proceed, because the Styrofoam's been gone a couple of weeks. And we never managed to identify the perpetrator in the first place."

"Channel that rage, Captain, we need to reassess the threat level and prioritise the investigation. I'll do that. But I need you to get to the Administrative Office right away and figure out a way to trace the thief. I'll send you the help you need. Once we get a hold of him, we might be able to get some answers. I don't need to impress the seriousness of this matter upon you, do I?"

"No, sir, you don't," the Chief of Security replies with a sharp salute.

When No. 2 appears on screen, he has his Bible and rosaries in hand. "Chief...?" He begins but recovering quickly, adds, "How may I help?"

"Sorry for interrupting your Bible study, No. 2, but it'll get a lot worse once you find out why. You remember the Styrofoam that was stolen?"

A little annoyed to find his calls going directly to the mailbox, the Chief Administrator leaves William a terse message. After pacing about the living room for a bit, he steps to his door and opens it to find Jan standing guard outside. "It's you on the shift again today," he says with a smile. "There's something I need you to do."

Even though Jan knocks repeatedly after ringing the bell several times, it's a while before the door is unlocked and a dishevelled William answers. "Administrative Associate Yuen," the peacekeeper sticks to protocol, "the Chief Administrator requests your presence at the Administrative Office immediately."

William blinks through a daze as he inquires, "Right now?"

"Ja," Jan responds. "He tried calling you, then had me look for you on the grid. I didn't see your RFID blip so I knew you had to be home."

"Who is it, Will?" they hear Paige call out. Recognizing the familiar voice, Jan breaks into a grin but says nothing as William sheepishly steps out and closes the door behind him. "Right now?" he asks a second time.

"Ja," Jan replies. "And I need your confirmation of having received this message from the Chief Administrator so I can report back to him."

"Alright, I understand. I'll be there as soon as I can, uh, I mean immediately," William replies, straightening himself up and waits for the peacekeeper to march away before letting himself back in.

When William arrives at the Administrative Office, he finds No. 2 sitting in the deserted waiting area and the Chief of Security pacing the corridors.

"Ah, William," No. 2 says with a wane smile. "You're here."

The Chief of Security doesn't appear as forgiving but says nothing.

"So, uh, why are we here?" William asks, unsure of himself for once.

"You remember the Styrofoam robbery, don't you?" the Chief of Security starts off in his harsh briefing room voice. "Turns out, you can make napalm with Styrofoam. Now that strange incident has become a matter of terrarium-wide concern. We've got to trace and grab it before it's deployed."

"Sounds good," William replies, now up to speed, coming off a little cocky.

"Only problem son, is that we don't have any leads, clues or suspects. Just witness statements that give us jackshit."

"Why don't we start by watching them again," No. 2 softly interjects. "There may be something we may have missed, you see."

"Fine! My station," the Chief of Security growls.

Once there, they pull up chairs from the adjoining office space and settle down. A few clicks later, the witness statements start to play. The Chief of Security has already viewed them, as has No. 2 but it's William's first time and he borrows a pad and a pen from the desk to make notes. The statements play out, Mrs Katzoff's first, followed by Kilia's and then Jhonatan's but the pad remains blank.

"Unfortunately," the Chief of Security says, breaking the heavy silence, "we don't have any training in crime detection in the program, but even Sherlock frickin' Holmes would have had his hands full with something like this."

William, rising to the challenge, ventures a question. "So, how exactly do you turn Styrofoam into napalm?"

"That's simple," the Chief of Security replies. "Just add gasoline."

A smile appears on William's face as he says, "So that's where we'll start."

#LetThereBeLove   **Follow** •••

What a day it's been... actually, what a fortnight...

So William went out there a few days after I did. And he got me a pretty plant from the zone. It really does brighten up the office and thankfully no one made a fuss.

No. 2 was all smiles and winks when he noticed it on my table. I guess he figured it out and he's cool with it.

So yea, William said he loved the meatloaf and this was his way of thanking me for it.

When he noticed me watering the plant a few days later, he invited me over to his place for an authentic home cooked Chinese meal, and well, waiting around at the shopping zones in Tower Twelve isn't as much fun as it used to be, so I said yes.

When I walked into his apartment today, I was hit by this weird earthy smell. William was quick to pop open the windows. HE HAS WINDOWSSSS!!! He said it was from the cooking. And I guess the second thing that struck me after a while was that he was like a totally different person.

He was talking a LOT, flipping from one thing to the next, laughing most of the time, and when he wasn't laughing, he had this shit eating grin on his face.

The Moo Shu Pork was delish! And we had some blush wine as well.

The plan was to Netflix & Chill, but after looking around for a bit, we ended up watching some funny videos on YouTube. I guess all that wine made them funnier. And then he was like, 'I'll show you something if you promise to not tell anyone'.

The auto-tuned one of the Chief Administrator he made from CCTV footage was HILARIOUS!! He even got the pen-clicks and everything.

His YouTube channel has a whole bunch of videos. His projects, as he calls them.

It was probably the wine talking when I said 'I'd love to be one of your projects.' That's when he leaned over and kissed me. He was

 **#LetThereBeLove**   **Follow** •••

tentative at first but grew bolder as we went along. The way he traced my lips with his tongue between kisses was just...

I'm glad he didn't have protection, who knows how far we might have gone.

So yea, I'm still at his apartment. He wasn't sure about when he'd return. I think I'll leave him a message and get going.

#SelfAwareIdiot #AllShookUp

60 DAYS AGO

20

Earthlings, All

"Good-morning, children!" Kilia says with a bright smile. "We're precisely half-way through the camp. Everyone good? Anyone have anything to share?" The days at Tweenland almost always started like this. Over time, realizing this was safe space, the kids had begun opening up to the group. Today, they're all seated on their mats, traces of smiles on their lips, expectant looks on their faces as they peer up at Josh and Kilia at the head of the room, but not one child utters a word.

"Any questions, then?" Josh asks.

An untainted child, hand raised, pipes up from the back right away, "What movie are we watching today?" All of the previous week, the children had started their day off with one of six carefully curated films which included, 'If You Build It' and 'Dancing In Jaffa' among others, and then spent a considerable part of the rest of the day in a guided discussion on what they had seen.

Poo, for one, was particularly taken up with 'The Sound of Music' and had been singing the farewell song to Josh and Kilia from the film on her way out every day since.

"We're done watching movies, kids," Josh answers. "But we will be watching videos on history, cultures and the arts in the last week of the camp."

"No movie?! That sucks!" the Cooper kid exclaims from the front.

"Actually kids, this is where the real fun begins," Kilia says immediately, before that knee-jerk response registers on the rest of the group. "All this time, you've been listening. Now, you'll be doing the listening and the talking. Would you like to know what we're going to start our discussions with?" Seeing that she hasn't lost her counselees' interest, she adds, "Our topic for today is—what it means to be human."

As Josh writes the words on the white-board, Kilia repeats, "What does it mean to be a human?" Some of the children keep looking right at her, unsure, while others look at the words on the board, a distant look in their eyes. "C'mon kids, what does it mean to be a human?" Kilia prompts with an encouraging smile. "There are no wrong answers here, just go ahead and tell us what you feel makes you human."

"What makes me human?" the Cooper kid asks. And getting a nod from Kilia, he answers, "To not be mutated. As God intended."

Well aware that this is a make or break moment, as much for the Cooper kid as the others, Kilia leans into this unplanned object lesson on free-speech and tolerance hard with, "Alright. Josh, could you write 'As God Intended' on the board, please? Would anyone else like to try?"

After finishing, Josh turns around and notices most of the mutated children and some of the untainted ones shift uncomfortably in their seats.

But Kilia stands her ground, saturnine.

The children, the Cooper kid included, furtively glance from Kilia to Josh and back to Kilia, the silence getting more oppressive with each passing second. *It's too soon to be doing this Kilia,* Josh thinks to himself as he sees her wordlessly pressing the children for a response with eye-contact, and turns back to the board, marker at the ready.

"I'm here for the falafel, y'all,

Don't holler at me bout no God,

The writing's on the wall. Human?

If that's you, dog, I'm glad I'm not."

Just as the Head Counsellor had lined up the Careers Day for the troubled mutated tween who had made all the drawings in black only, she also had a one-on-one session with the mutated tween whose rap had resonated with No. 2 and encouraged him to develop his spoken-word skills. He'd been unstoppable since.

Josh doesn't restrain the smile welling up inside him, knowing the children can't see his face and after waiting for Kilia to paraphrase the caustic response but hearing nothing, scrawls 'Falafel' on the board.

The children break out in laughter and Kilia, thankful the tension in the room has been cut yet not wanting to lose momentum, persists gently, "How about you, Poo, what makes you human?"

"I don't know," Poo replies, rising slowly. "I don't want to be human..."

"You don't?" the Cooper kid blurts in shock.

"My mum got me a VR set for my birthday, to learn and play when she is at work and I'm home by myself. I started watching a nature show about how humans changed the planet. As humans arrived on each continent, the other species would start to go extinct..." Tears start to well up in Poo's eyes and she just stands there, helpless.

"And...?" Josh asks, overcome with curiosity.

"When I told my mum about it, she called customer support

and now I can't find the show anymore. My mum says I have to wait till I'm older to watch the rest."

"When you get to see it, sweetie, you'll see that we humans realized the impact we were having on our environment and did all we could to save it," Kilia soothes. "How about we replace 'Human' with another word we like better," she adds to get the discussion back on track, "that sound good?"

As Josh begins wiping the white-board without needing to be told, the children, all of them now engaged in the discussion, begin contributing—person, being, things that walk on two legs, living thing, organism.

Kilia takes in the full range of non-verbal reactions from the children as Josh writes each word. Seeing Poo still standing, even after they're all out, she asks, "Do you have a favourite from the new words, sweetie?" But Poo shakes her head from side to side.

"How about Earthling," Josh proposes. And Poo transforms into her usual self again.

"Kids, I hope you enjoyed the discussion we had today," Kilia brings the day at Tweenland to an end. "And boys," she continues, turning to directly address the Cooper kid and the rapping mutant tween, "Don't forget your special assignment for tomorrow."

"Have a good evening," Josh adds as the children file out of the room and Poo begins her adorable, even if slightly off-key rendition of 'So long, farewell'. "And you earthlings who have started taking the antidote to get your baseline levels established," Kilia reminds the untainted children in her care, "take it with a smile. I know it hurts. But we're all in it together, aren't we?"

"Tomorrow should be interesting," Josh remarks, after the daily report has been filed, and the last of the all-purpose mats have been rolled up.

"I'm a little anxious myself," Kilia admits. "Getting the kids, especially ones like those two, to list out the similarities and differences between untainted survivors and mutated humans works better when we're done with..."

"When we're supposed to!" Josh interjects with a laugh. And adds, "But they're earthlings now, so I think that should be fine."

"I was improvising!" Kilia retorts. "Like you were with the falafel thing. And earthlings, genius!"

"Do you need any help getting the toys for tomorrow's geometric psych session?" Josh asks, hoping to spend just a little more time with her.

"I'm sure Sebastian uncle must be waiting for you," she replies, sorry to see him go. "I know you think you're a squiggly, but you strike me as a circle," the words escape her lips. And she hastily adds, "I know those were the results you got, but over 83% of mutated humans test that way. Probably the result of life in the Quarantine Zone on the psyche. My theory is: the shape they would originally relate to has been subsumed by the squiggly. I'm thinking of writing a paper on it."

"Subsumed...?" Josh asks.

"Imagine a circle, with the squiggly wrapped around it."

"Something like a globe constricted by a boa?" Seeing her otherwise steady eyes widen, Josh smilingly adds, "And before you start analysing that visual, Counsellor, you should know, it was the logo of the 'New Left', some sort of a socialist group or something. I saw it on their newsletter. And the globe had a twig and a leaf. I'm not whether it was meant to look like an apple or a pear…"

"And where did you get your hands on that?"

"At my place. In the Quarantine Zone." Josh replies with a slight shrug. "There are all sorts of books in there."

"Really? I'd love to see it someday."

Knowing that would never come to pass, Josh smiles through downcast eyes.

The Chief Administrator's doing his transcendental meditation right now, and Will's taking the time to psych himself before his big presentation. Jeez! He's been at it for nights.

Ever since he stumbled upon that picture of the 'Comply' graffiti on the Great Wall of China, he's been obsessing, like, all over it. Sheesh! What a buzz-kill. But it's trippy alright cos it appeared in a bunch of places in different parts of the world, and that too nearly three decades ago.

But last night things got way out of hand.

I woke up when I realized he wasn't next to me and found him at his desk outside. Vaping as always and watching a video on 'The Mandela Effect.' So there's this Hadron Collider McGuffin that speeds up atoms to rip through space and time and a bunch of sciencey shit I just didn't get.

And then he began totally wigging out over a Facebook page for a book. Something to do with Carols and Reactors *facepalm*. He was totes tripping balls. Wait, am I repeating myself. He's going viral and he's infecting me as well but I just had to listen when he said that we might all be characters in a work of fiction.

My Christianity was put to the test so I kept my inner bitch in check and said nothing more than 'You're high af Will, come to bed.'

I guess the investigation is stressing him out. At this point, tho, I'd even be willing to try an exorcism.

Who am I kidding, it's probably the MaryJane. I've got to get him to kick the habit.

But I'll have to figure out a way to do that without him catching on.

cues Wonder Woman Theme #GurlPower #GameOnBitches

21

The Mutie, The Beast
and the Three Wise Men

A rickety bus sputters to a halt at the terminal near the marketplace. A curious trio, each bearing improvised jute backpacks filled to capacity with produce from the fields, rise from their seats. "Thank you for that sweet ride, Mr Bus Driver," the blind one says cheerily, as he makes his way to the exit at the front, one hand on the shoulder of the dumb one. "Thank you, young man, but I'm a woman," the driver replies. "And like 'ol Bessie here," she adds as she lovingly caresses the steering wheel, "I've seen better days myself."

Hearing the first of what is bound to be a long exchange, the dumb one grabs the deaf one who's about to disembark and pulls him back, signing furiously. "He's doing it again. You know the rules. He gets talky, he's yours." The blind one, so happy to make a new acquaintance, barely notices the changing of the guide as he babbles on.

Luxuriating in the dull roar afforded to him by the terminal, a welcome change from the verbal diarrhoea he was subjected to for the entire duration of the ride, the dumb one looks about with mild disinterest. But seeing a crowd gathering at one of the corners, he languidly saunters in its general direction.

The blind one is still yammering away when the dumb one sticks his head into the bus, gesticulating wildly, the excitement evident on his face.

"You think I don't want this over with?" the deaf one signs back in response. "But we let him run his mouth off now, it'll be much quieter later on."

"Something super cool is going on at the corner," the dumb one signs back. "Let's get moving, because it'll probably be over soon."

"Mother of Christ, isn't that Councilman David?" the deaf one remarks as they make their way through the crowd. "Wonder what he's doing here."

"Councilman David? At this hour? Dayumn!" The blind one perks up, adding, "And that smell..." as he starts sniffing. "Wait... Don't tell me..."

"Spray paint!!" he declares triumphantly, after taking a few more sniffs. "What I say?"

Getting no response, he adds nervously, "Don't leave me hanging now... What's happenin?"

"Tell him!" the dumb one signs to the deaf one. And the deaf one announces, "A bunch of kids are painting. The Councilman's talking to a camera. That's it. Bada bing! *Andosh!*"

"Seriously?" The dumb one signs to the deaf one, excruciating incredulity on his face.

Rolling his eyes and sighing, the deaf one begins again, "You remember the graffiti I was telling you about, the 'Comply' graffiti? With the peacekeeper man? Turns out, it's some sort of a UN thing. They're inviting everyone to participate and like I said, a bunch of kids are at it." Turning to the dumb one, he adds, "Happy?"

As they make their way to the church, the dumb one keeps prodding the deaf one to describe every little detail he was struck by. Barely have they stepped through the gate, when he signs, "We should tell Pastor Felipe, I'm sure he'd love to see it too."

"He's leading the choir practice right now, brothers," the blind one, having picked up the harmonies long before the other two can, answers after the deaf one has voiced the thought. "He needs his music right now. The tax-man's been testing his faith."

The conference room is dark but for the screen where William stands, the colourful pie-chart partially projected on his shirt. Knowing full well that he's making the most absurd presentation of his life, he has overcompensated by culling and visualizing data from Reddit and 4Chan threads among others and cited no sources, just in case the Chief Administrator decides to Google them. "By comparison," William begins concluding his big-data analysis, "the reverse image search on the 'Comply' graffiti on live pages got far fewer hits. But here are the numbers of archived pages from the 'Wayback Machine'. It's hard to say if and when this imagery began trending, and looking into that may not even be relevant but I'm sure we can send requests for police records. It may be time consuming but the high-profile sites that were tagged, like the 'Taj Mahal' – much like the 'Great Wall', would have certainly been investigated. And if any of them ended with a successful prosecution, we may even have someone to question."

The Chief Administrator, his face hidden in the shadows, had been deathly silent all this while, his pen clicks conspicuous by their absence.

"I'm sure we've crossed the point where data patterns start looking like white noise, sir," William resorts to levity.

"Perhaps we should jump to the executive summary."

Taking her cue, Paige brightens the room and the lights, as they come on, both reveal the Chief Administrator taking a power-nap and bring him to life as well.

"Sorry, William," the Chief Administrator yawns nonchalantly, and massages the back of his neck. "You lost me when you started off with your Axioms of Probability, Regression Analysis mumbo jumbo."

"But Chief Administrator... If the universe is conspiring..." William blurts, somehow managing to hide the shock on his face from everyone except Paige.

"The universe, young William, is an old man with a beard who drives his cab badly," the Chief Administrator pronounces with finality. "I suggest you spend your time focusing on the investigation. But that quote you opened with—Only the paranoid survive—that was good, I might use it." Turning to Paige, he continues, "Alright then, what do we have next?"

No. 2 isn't as quick to leave the conference room as his superior. And seeing William busy himself powering down the projector and computer, meticulously coiling and putting the cables away, he stays until it's just the two of them left. Gently placing his hand on the humiliated young man's shoulder, he says, "Forgive him. He does that sometimes."

He's at the door of the conference room when William finally speaks.

"Councilman David has been commissioned to shoot a video, No. 2. Our so-called PR exercise. Everyone at H.Q. will see it soon enough. If this blows up..."

"You did your part, William. What happens now is between Him and His god."

"Our man on the inside," Viktor addresses the tall man in the green scrubs who had been silent for most of the meeting. "They ask him many questions, many times..."

"So they're conducting an investigation. There was bound to be some heat," one of the others standing in the operation theatre replies. "Why are we surprised?"

"No... No surprise. I thought it was funny. First questions. Then stress test. Then more questions. Then they make voice recording." Spoilt by his years of prepotency, this is Viktor standing, hat in hand. "Is like American Idol, yes?" he adds with forced sarcasm.

"Stress test? They made him run on a treadmill?" The portly gent in the viewing gallery asks, reaching for his spectacles. "What would that accomplish?"

"Maybe they're on to something or maybe they're just fishing," the surgeon resumes. "Either way, we have no control over the schedule so we just have to sit tight. Your contact, Viktor, he's keeping it together, right?"

"He starting to get twitchy. I offer to unload some Krokodil on his sister, but he say she never go for that."

"Then there's nothing more to do but wait," the tall surgeon finally speaks, the ring of defeat in his voice in stark contrast with his raised fist. As the others begin to raise their fists in the air, Viktor swallows his pride and pleads, "Can't we do something for the sister? Something small also ok. Slightly less old computer or maybe little more comfortable chair?"

"A chair?" the tall surgeon asks, counting on his words to do the damage as his despair laden tone evokes empathy. "We're all probably questioning our collective wisdom in backing your plans and schemes so far, Viktor. That street-art project of yours which was to drive disenfranchised youth to us in droves, those very kids who should have been here with us now have been bought off with a few cans of paint. Your intentions were never in doubt but we can't afford to confuse the means with the ends anymore."

"When the Pharaohs enslave us to build their pyramids," Aiko shrieks, rising to Viktor's defence, "are we wrong in marking our doorposts with the blood of lambs?"

Both the tall surgeon and Viktor lower their gaze. Viktor, in resignation, the tall surgeon to contain the slightest gleam that might give him away.

44 DAYS AGO

22

The Public Trial

The Grand Arena in Tower One is nearly packed yet stragglers continue walking in. All untainted survivors as well as mutated humans above the age of eighteen had been invited via the Daily Bulletin that aired inside the terrarium and over the Chief Administrator's fire-side chat in the Quarantine Zone. Their curiosity piqued, everyone who could afford to miss half a day's work to be here, is.

Dropping Tidjane off at Sebastian's, who had volunteered to baby-sit so that both Khady and Alasco could attend, took a little longer than expected. They're not as close to the dais as they'd like to be but still close enough to one of the many large screens that display a video feed of the proceedings, so they're content in the knowledge that they won't miss out on much. They stand quietly in mild apprehension for their daughter, waiting for the trial to begin, listening in on bits and pieces of the conversations from the people around.

"I've never been here before. Have you?" they hear someone say.

"This arena has been put to use at this scale only once before. That was when the Terrarium was formally inaugurated. Everyone had been invited back then, just like today," another voice replies.

"Was it this packed back then?"

"Oh, I don't think so, because we didn't have as many volunteers. We have more people from the old world migrating each year so our numbers have gone up."

"Do you think this turnout, especially the large numbers of the mutants, has something to do with the gravity of the incident? It was an armed robbery, after all."

"It's not like a mutated human was involved. The first bulletin we saw about the Styrofoam Incident was pretty clear on that."

Just then, the Deputy Chief Administrator steps on the dais which gets lit to full intensity and the crowd gradually falls silent.

"Ladies and gentlemen, thank you for being here today," his voice rings out from the powerful speakers adjoining the stage and from the smaller speakers that accompany the screens placed at strategic points in the grand arena. "The administration has carried out a thorough investigation and built a case for the prosecution. Our Chief Administrator will preside and a jury comprising six untainted survivors and six mutated humans, already picked by lottery, will deliberate." Turning towards the wing at the far side with his hand extended, he continues, "The Chief Administrator and the members of the jury."

As the Chief Administrator and the jury walk on stage and take their seats, the Chief Administrator at the dead centre with the jury on one side, they are met with a scattered and awkward applause.

"Some of you may be wondering how to conduct yourself at this event," No. 2 continues, his grim face filling the video screens as David zooms in on a close up. "Suffice it to say we take this matter very seriously and request you to do the same."

David, who had been specifically called in to supervise the entire production, directs the cinematographer to switch to a long shot so that both the audience away from the stage and the UN delegates who will eventually view the recording, get the big picture.

"Ever since the Styrofoam Incident," the Chief Administrator begins as No. 2 walks offstage, "we racked our heads over why anyone would take such extreme measures. That too, over packing-materials." Reassuringly, he adds, "Steps have been taken to ensure that nothing of this sort happens again, of course, but when we realized that Styrofoam could be used to make napalm, it transformed into a much more critical matter." He pauses, just enough to let his words sink in, savouring the collective gasp. "And so, here we are, to ensure that this one robbery doesn't escalate into anything more troubling."

Taking his cue from the barely audible pen-click, No. 2 announces from the wings, "And now, the witnesses for the prosecution."

As Kilia, Jhonatan, Mrs Katzoff and the Chief of Security make their entrance, David directs the videographer to track them as they enter and sit on one side of the jury.

Unannounced, William is the last to appear on stage. "Upon your beliefs," he gets to it right away, "upholding all you consider sacred, do you swear to tell the truth, the whole truth and nothing but the truth, so help you God?"

"We do," the witnesses respond in unison.

"The administration calls upon the first witness, the Chief of Security for the Terrarium and the greater Diablo area," No. 2 announces from the wings.

"Is it true, sir, that you serve as the Chief of Security at Eden (925)?" William begins his line of questioning. "And when the incident occurred, the perpetrator got away with all the Styrofoam he could get without leaving a trace?"

"That is correct," the Chief of Security replies.

"Could you elaborate?"

"Well, the perp wasn't carrying his RFID credit card so he didn't register on the grid. The mask he was wearing, amateurish as it was, got the job done. The knife he used to take Mrs Katzoff hostage was standard issue. You'd find one in every household in the Terrarium. He then disappeared down the interconnected basements of the tower complex. And the mask – in all probability, it was burnt and disposed."

"So how did you go about finding the needle from the proverbial haystack?"

A wry smile appears on the Chief of Security's face as he answers because it was his own passing reference that William had based their entire strategy on. "As you suggested, the night we learnt that Styrofoam could be used to make napalm, we did so by elimination. First, we made a comprehensive list of suspects by cross referencing all males who were off-grid at the time with all personnel who had access to gasoline. We also included truck drivers who had been getting lower mileage and could have been pilfering fuel steadily. This gave us a list of a little over 4,500 which was then trimmed down by taking away all those with credible alibis. And trimmed down, again, by taking away those that did not match the physical description. This left us with about 300 probables."

"Thank you, sir," William says, relieved that the Chief of Security hadn't fudged a single rehearsed word.

"Our second witness, Jhonatan Gunarsa," No. 2 announces, "was manning the check-out counter at the hypermarket when the robbery took place."

William steps towards Jhonatan and continues, "Is it true,

Mr Gunarsa, that you provided the most comprehensive physical description of the perpetrator and it was this physical description that was used to bring down the list of probable perpetrators from about 300 to 60?"

"Yes, that's right," Jhonatan replies.

"Could you repeat the description you gave to the peacekeepers when you were recording your statement?"

"Of course, la. He was about 5′ 7″, medium build and looked like he weighed 175 pounds. Also, by his skin tone—I could tell since he wasn't wearing gloves—he was brown skinned. Brown-eyed as well. With tinges of grey. At the time I gave my statement, I thought he must have been Latino, but later when they showed me a shade card, I was able to identify a specific range of tones for both skin and retina."

"So, did that widen or narrow the search for the perpetrator?" William asks.

"It may have widened the range in terms of ethnicity, but I'm sure the range of browns I picked must have helped. I'm good with colours."

"They did, Mr Gunarsa, thank you."

"Our third witness, Kilia Bagyoko. She was present at the time of the robbery," No. 2 announces.

"Miss Bagyoko, in your first statement at the security checkpost, you mentioned that the perpetrator had a unique raspy voice that got high-pitched when he was screaming."

Seeing Kilia nod timidly, William prompts, "We need a verbal answer for the record, Miss."

"Sorry... he had... it did... I mean… that is correct."

"So, when you heard the recordings of the 60 odd probables, did any sound like the perpetrator?" William asks, his even tone masking the thrill he feels at how well he's made the case so far, both in terms of detection and presentation, especially because the proceedings would be viewed by the higher-ups at H.Q. "And if so, how many voices did you believe matched the perpetrator's?"

"Three voices, there were three that were very similar to the voice of the man who held up the hypermarket with his knife. Of those, one was exactly like his."

"Thank you, Miss Bagyoko."

"Our last witness, Mrs Katzoff. She was held at knifepoint by the robber," No. 2 announces.

"Mrs Katzoff, the robber, the one who held you at knifepoint, was he sweating profusely and emitting a distinct body odour?" William asks.

"Oy vey... That fershtinkiner..." Mrs Katzoff replies, coming to life, "They could smell him in Shamayim and Sheol!"

"I will take that as a yes," William continues. "And is it true that you were given three swabs from which you had to choose the one closest to that odour?"

"When those peacekeepers gave me those disgusting rags, everyone makes jokes about our noses, I thought they were putting my shnoz to the test. And who knows what they had to do to get all that sweat on those rags..."

"Mrs Katzoff," William interrupts. "If you could answer the question..."

"I'm sorry, what was the question?"

"Were you able to identify the odour?" William asks, skipping ahead to assuage his mounting impatience.

"Of course! It took me less than a second to identify the one. I'll never forget it for as long as I breathe, it was a very distinct, acrid..."

"That will be all, Mrs Katzoff," William interrupts again, and bowing slightly towards all four witnesses, adds, "Thank you for your testimony."

"We now call upon Mr Harish Goel," No. 2 announces. "A migrant from India. He volunteered at the Diablo UN mission to be close to his elder sister."

David, amazed as he is by the administration's tenacious investigation, directs the cinematographer nonetheless to cut to a wide shot as the accused is led onto the stage by two peacekeepers. "Now start zooming in slowly, and time it so that we're on a tight close-up by the time he gets to the stand," David whispers, praying his subject lets some usable emotion slip through.

After swearing Harish in, William begins his questioning in rapid-fire. "Is it true, Mr Goel, that you were home when the incident occurred?"

"Yes, that is true."

"Given that you live in the domicile assigned to you alone, you have no way of proving it."

"Yes... unfortunately..."

"As a transport vehicle operator, you have access to gasoline and your truck has been getting significantly lesser mileage than other trucks that have been in service for just as long despite regular maintenance and other measures taken by the mechanics."

"Yes, that is correct but I am... I was a teacher, I don't understand these things. I just drive the truck."

"You'd forgive us for thinking you've been pilfering gasoline for private profit, wouldn't you?"

"It wouldn't be fair. Understandable maybe, but not fair," Harish asserts weakly. "But that is not the case."

"Alright, if you insist. But this isn't about the pilfered gasoline.

It's about the Styrofoam. Now isn't it true that you match the physical description down to the T, and both your voice and your body odour have been positively identified?"

Harish's tone is despondent as he admits, "Yes…"

"All the evidence we have uncovered, even while it implicates you in the crime, it could be dismissed in a courtroom as circumstantial," William feints before swooping in for the kill. "You have no representation either. But you are the only suspect still standing from a list of 4,500. So, I ask you. Upon all you hold sacred, did you do it? Did you hold up the hypermarket, take Mrs Katzoff – a senior citizen of our terrarium hostage and steal all that Styrofoam?"

Harish stands immobile, his eyes downcast. But his face in close-up on all the screens in the arena leaves no room for doubt in the minds of those present.

"Are you a part of a group involved in making napalm, Mr Goel?" William ups the ante. "This isn't just about you or the Styrofoam any more. And you will be treated with leniency should you cooperate. So, I ask you again, did you do it?"

Unable to sustain the onslaught, the mild-mannered middle-aged man mumbles, "No, and I have nothing more to say."

"I'm sorry, but could you come again?" William presses on, now beginning to hate himself a little.

The Chief Administrator chooses that very moment to ostensibly make notes and clicks his pen to life. On cue, the Deputy Chief Administrator's voice rings out from the wings. "We now call upon Anamika Goel, the sister of the accused. An I.T. professional, she was on a consulting project in the Bay Area when the apocalypse took place. She now works as a secretary at the Council for Mutant Affairs."

Seeing Harish aghast, a self-satisfied look appears on the Chief Administrator's face but only for a fleeting moment.

"Ma'am, as you have not been called to testify," William keeps the show going, "you will not be sworn in. But I hope you will side with the greater good. In light of all the facts and evidence presented here today, do you have anything you'd like to say?"

Anamika glares at William with consternation, but the shame in her voice is louder, "I would like to speak to my brother directly. May I?"

A little stumped, William turns to the Chief Administrator who nods benignly.

"Please go ahead, ma'am."

"Hari...?" Anamika asks, her consternation now unleashed.

"They were going to make your job redundant..." the accused speaks haltingly through his tears after a few moments, his eyes still downcast. "They would have you work in the fields... You were always the fragile one... I couldn't let you suffer any more than you already were."

As a murmur reverberates through the audience, William, guiding the hand of one conscientious fool, hammers the last nail in the coffin of the other. "Mr Goel, are we to understand that you did it to protect your sister?"

"Hari! Answer him!"

43 DAYS AGO

23

Punishment! Punishment!

"Good-morning Kilia," the children echo in their sing-song chorus.

"Where were you yesterday?" the Cooper kid asks and Poo softly adds, "We missed you."

"Kids, there was a robbery in the terrarium," having picked up on Kilia's vulnerable state before the children arrived, Josh answers on her behalf. "And since she happened to be a witness, she had been called to testify. But it wasn't so bad, was it? We got to spend the day with the Head Counsellor." Turning to Kilia, he whispers, "She'd like a word."

"Forget that boring hag!

The cat's outta the bag 'bout the apocalypse,

But we still here, ain't we?

Shine the light on the robbery, we'll deal,

With the truth, yo, set us free," the mutant tween freestyles.

Getting an encouraging nod from Josh, Kilia begins reluctantly, "A masked man held up the hypermarket, you know the one we had visited earlier. I happened to be there at the time."

"He broke the eighth commandment!" the Cooper kid

exclaims. "He should be punished."

"So, this man," Kilia continues with a sigh, "he needed all the Styrofoam they had. He was forced to hold an old lady at knifepoint because Styrofoam isn't available anywhere except..."

"He was willing to break the sixth commandment too?" The Cooper kid interrupts. "He has got to be punished!" And taking it even further, he begins riling the other children up by chanting, "Punishment! Punishment! Punishment!"

"No children... simmer down..." Kilia pleads helplessly. "If you were there, you'd have seen he wasn't a bad man. Only a man who found himself in a bad situation with very few choices." But seeing her words take no effect, she turns to Josh.

"Kids!" Josh roars, bringing the clamour to a screeching halt. The children, never having seen this side of Josh before, stare at him with terror in their eyes.

Knowing Kilia is in no position to help, flummoxed himself, Josh starts by clutching at straws, "Alright, alright. Rules are important. Each game we play comes with its own set of rules, right? And we shouldn't break them, right? Can anyone tell me why not?"

"Because we get punished if we do?" a child from the back squeaks.

Responses of this sort usually evoked spontaneous laughter and the exchange of knowing glances among the kids, but now the children all wince in anticipation.

Deliberately settling into a squatting position near the kids at the edge of the mats, Josh begins speaking in a soft, almost conspiratorial voice. "You remember how Poo was telling us that each time humans moved to a continent, other species were driven to extinction?" Responding predictably to the abrupt change of topic, body language and intonation, the children all lean forward, fear replaced by curiosity.

"That happened because of our big brains," Josh continues, tapping his temple with his index finger, a gentle smile on his face. "Because not only can we work together towards a common goal, we've been given the gift of language. It's like a super-power. It allows us to communicate, share ideas. And among other things, curtail conflict with the help of rules."

The doctor's words from a discussion they'd had on a day of rest not too long ago, now flow smoothly. "It bolstered the evolutionary advantage of social living. It's not like we wanted to drive other species extinct; it was just a by-product of our continued existence. Apart from their meat, we used their skin, leather and bones to get by. Over time, we developed substitutes that were far easier to manufacture. That economic factor, coupled with their already depleting numbers added to the rarity and animal products, especially fur, became status symbols. But then rules were framed to protect those very species we were driving extinct."

"As we grow, kids, not just as individuals but as a society on the whole, we know better," Kilia says, now joining the discussion. "And we make new rules, change the old ones. Because rules exist to serve us. Not the other way around."

"One of the greatest things about this country, children, is our constitution." Josh continues, still retracing the journey the Doctor had taken him on and glad to be helped along by Kilia. "Sort of like the rule book for the nation. It was neither the first of its kind, nor did it spell everything out in excessive detail, like, say the constitution of India..."

"But it has been amended," Kilia interrupts, starting to enjoy the banter. "To reflect the change in our collective conscience over time. For example, slavery was abolished by the 13th Amendment."

"Yes, but we abide by the rules until they're changed, no?" Josh retorts with a smile.

"Yes," Kilia admits. "The man broke the law, put a senior citizen in danger. One who was supported by a productive family, out of love. But if the man's sister's reaction was anything to go by, I'm sure he must have been conflicted about his actions as well."

"So, what will happen to him?" Poo asks, a look of concern on her face.

"That is something for the jury to decide, sweetie, and for the UN to ratify or supersede. But he did commit a crime. He will have to account for it," Kilia answers, the sadness back in her voice.

"Punishment! Punishment! Punishment!" the Cooper kid starts rallying once again, but this time the chant doesn't quite take as it did before.

"So kids, we have a surprise for you," Kilia says, after the children have quietened down without further intervention. "Today, for the first time in a camp for you pre-teen earthlings, we have a Careers Day lined up. While we wait for our guests to arrive, we're going to start by telling you about our jobs. As you all know, Josh and I, we're both child counsellors."

"We've received training to help us assist you with this transition you're making right now," Josh adds. "While I have only a basic understanding of child psychology, Kilia has her Masters from a well-established and grounded university."

"So how come you two do the same job?" the Cooper kid asks.

"The thing is, children, life in a UN mission, just like anyplace else, is subject to supply and demand," Kilia clarifies.

"My education didn't qualify me for a job as a Counsellor at the Hospital out in the Quarantine Zone," Josh adds with a smile. "But I guess the administration thought I'd do just fine with you earthlings. As for Kilia, she could have easily gotten a better paying position at another Terrarium, but she wanted to live close to her family here. The ones she lives for."

Just then, there's a knock on the door and Mr Cooper, Alasco and two mutated humans, of which one looks like he works in construction and another with no identifying accessories or uniform on her person, step in. "We're here for the Careers Day," Mr Cooper drawls. "Something the administration wants to try out?"

"Thank you, Mr Cooper. The children are ready and waiting," Kilia says, stepping forward with a welcoming smile on her face as Josh rises slowly. Turning to Josh, she adds, "I'll go meet the boss now. You'll manage, right?" Catching Alasco's eye, she leaves him with a quick, "Bye, Dad," on her way out.

By the time Kilia returns, she feels a lot more centred. Her eyes are a little red from the tears but the smile on her face isn't forced anymore. Seeing Josh powering the kids down for nap-time with the usual Shava-asana as she opens the door, she backs away into the foyer.

It isn't long before Josh steps out and sits alongside on the floor as they usually do each day, comparing notes while the children rest.

"So, how was it?" she asks.

Replying with one thumb up and a smile, Josh inquires, "And your session with the boss?"

"You mean 'that boring hag'?" Kilia bursts out laughing. "We really have to rein little Eminem in... So, she didn't tell me anything I didn't already know, but it's good to hear those things from another."

"The Millennials thought they had it tough," Kilia begins thoughtfully after a few moments have passed, "but our kids, they're going to grow up and be faced with some really impossible choices. What that man did for his sister, I would've done for Djane. He'd probably do the same for me."

His better judgement giving way to instinct, Josh gently places his hand on Kilia's.

"I really hope we're doing our part right." Caught unawares mid-sentence, Kilia feels the burden she'd been carrying since the robbery melt away. And in the ensuing bliss, she finds herself unable to form even a single sentence.

"And what were you saying about the rules earlier?" she manages a throaty whisper, as she turns her palm upwards and entwines her fingers with his.

Feeling his pulse race, his fur stand on edge, he starts breathing deep to regain control. Doing his best to expunge the emotion. But seeing her do the same, he gently pulls back. "We'll have to wait for an amendment."

41 DAYS AGO

24

Overheard

"The Auditors will be here again tomorrow and who knows what else they'll bite into, what more they'll take a slice of." Pastor Felipe frets, oblivious to the gastronomic references he makes as he paces up and down the backroom which has been converted into a kitchen.

It is late in the evening and three of his volunteers are busy preparing for the last of the day's batch of rolls. Despite their impairment due to the mutation, they do their jobs steadily. The deaf one chops the lettuce, the dumb one fries the falafel balls and the blind one stands stirring the hummus pot.

The amusement that Pastor Felipe usually derives, seeing them at work as they go over the day's events in their own unique manner, is not in the least bit unkind. But today is different. The Pastor has been testy all day. He stops abruptly, turns to face his flock and says, "I'd better go pray that they might go a little easy on us."

The dumb one signs this to the deaf one adding, "Thank you, God," who says this out loud for the blind one's ears, who, in turn, whoops a "Hallelujah" which the dumb one immediately signs to the deaf one.

"So the two of youse heard anything about the verdict? What they'll do with that untainted human?" the deaf one asks.

"Shiiiit," the blind one starts. "Sending his ass back to where he came from don't sound good to me either, but sending him out here? What kind of message the Administration be sending, recommending that second option to the jury?"

The dumb one, not really having an opinion on the matter, signs all of this to the deaf one, an ambivalent look on his face.

"Whaddya gonna do," the deaf one remarks. "But that mutie named in the confession?" Ducking just in time to avoid the falafel ball lobbed at him by the dumb one, he adds, "I'll break your arm, my friend!!"

"Mutant, please!" the blind one intercedes.

"So that *mutant* who allegedly forced him into committing the crime," the deaf one resumes. "What're they gonna do to him? He's livin' in the zone already for Christ's sake. Where are they going to send him off to? The moon?"

Aiko has been restless and fidgety in her seat in the viewing gallery throughout as the tall man in scrubs stands updating the participants about the response from their mysterious backer to the progress report he had delivered earlier in the day.

"Seriously?!" She shrieks abruptly. "Are we really going to keep sweating the small stuff instead of talking about Viktor, you disgusting cowards!!"

For a moment, no one speaks, then the tall man says soothingly, "Please calm down, Aiko. I was saving that part for the last. Everyone here, our backer included, mourn Viktor's passing and..."

"Mourn him? You had him put down because he was identified and could have been questioned. This is not a meeting of the resistance but of cold-blooded murderers! And cowards!"

"Look, Aiko," the surgeon continues. "No one can deny that the timing of his death was, to say the least, convenient to our cause. It warrants suspicion and we can barely begin to imagine how you must feel. But we were planning on hiding him in the outlying territories until we were ready to swing into action, not on... putting him down. His passing saddens us all..."

"Liar!" Aiko screams, refusing to back down.

"He was to lead the charge, Aiko. Don't you see? The sadness of his passing apart, we have to deal with the task of finding someone to replace him, if that's even possible." As the portly gent furiously polishes his spectacles, the tall man continues calmly, "Would you be up for it?"

"Hey, Doc," Josh says as he is let in. "How're you today?"

"Fine," Dr Hudson replies wearily, even though his appearance screams otherwise.

"You know, the mutant named by the Styrofoam thief? I overheard people on the bus," Josh begins right away. "They were saying his name was Viktor. The same Viktor I met here?"

"Maybe," the Doctor quietly replies, his face ashen. "But it doesn't matter; he's no longer with us."

"Did the administration take him for questioning?"

"He passed away at the hospital when he had gone for his weekly shot. Chemical interaction with some of the Krokodil he was flush with at the time, I suppose."

"But he must have known the risks, being a Krokodil merchant himself," Josh persists. "Don't you find it odd that the man named by the thief ends up dead soon after?"

"Look, son," Doctor Hudson replies. "I don't get out much

and what little I do know comes from the few who care to visit. It was Councilman David who told me. These deaths occur all the time because drug-induced chemical interactions or otherwise, the antidote hasn't been perfected yet and all of us suffering from radiation poisoning are constantly in flux to begin with. You're free to decide for yourself," he adds with a mournful finality. "I don't wish to discuss this anymore."

"Doctor?" Josh asks, seeing his mentor rise abruptly after a long awkward silence.

"I've got something on my hands, I'll be right back."

"So. What have you been reading?" the doctor asks upon his return.

"I found an interesting set of books with pictures and words," Josh begins excitedly. "The drawings show what's happening throughout, what the characters look like, and what they say is set in little bubbles with pointy tails linking it to the person who said the words. Like a play, I think."

"Graphic novels?" the Doctor asks with the hint of a smile. "Regular book-sized or are they slightly larger but a whole lot slimmer?"

"Larger and slimmer, Doc..."

"Comic books!!" Doctor Hudson exclaims with joy. "I used to love them in my youth. Who am I kidding, I still do. But back when the Marvel method of story-telling took the world by storm, those were the days! I have to admit, though, Stan Lee got more than his fair share of credit and fandom. His contemporaries and collaborators, Jack Kirby most of all, faded away unnoticed. Oh wait, what am I saying? You wouldn't know about the ridiculous cameos he began making in the movies his company co-produced. All strategically placed as well. Tell me about the stories, the comic books you're reading. Superheroes, right?"

"Yes, there are heroes," Josh replies, making a slashing move with an imaginary sword. "On both sides. Equally powerful villains too and they all use something called the Force as they battle one another."

"A long time ago in a galaxy far, far away?" the Doctor responds with delight. "Ooh the Jedi, the Sith, and their magnificent light sabres... you've got yourself a bunch of Star Wars comic books, son."

"Yes, I sort of got that much from what I've read so far," Josh says. "But I don't understand this Force thing. It's not for real, is it?"

"If only..." the doctor laughs. "I'd have mind-tricked my way into Tracy Chapman's pants, and then some. But there was this one philosopher whose central work, The World as Will and Representation, came quite close. He theorized that the world, all of nature, man even – has come about by and is an expression of an insatiable will to life."

"So that will, is that the Force the Jedi and Sith use to control things with their mind?"

"Perhaps," the Doctor replies. "But Schopenhauer predates Lucas by over a hundred and fifty years so I don't know what he'd have to say. On the other hand, multiple philosophical and religious concepts can be said to have influenced the themes we see in Star Wars. But coming back to the Force, as per canon, it's been described as an energy field created by all living things. It surrounds, penetrates and binds everything in the galaxy. Most die-hard fans would actually prefer comparisons to Qi or Chi, the life energy as described by ancient Chinese thinkers."

"Oh..." Josh says, a little awed by the intricacies of what he had devoured without a single thought. "Could you tell me some more... about the Will, or is it the Force... I... I think I'm getting lost here."

#NoobPhilos

OKAY, LET'S START WITH THE WILL, SON... WHILE SCHOPENHAUER DIDN'T DWELL ON WHO WAS PROJECTING THE WILL AND THUS BRINGING ABOUT THE REPRESENTATION HE BROKE IT DOWN INTO TWO: THE WILL THAT IS THE KANTIAN THING-IN-ITSELF; AND THE INDIVIDUAL WILLS OF HUMANS AND ANIMALS WHICH IN TURN ARE PHENOMENA OF THE OVERARCHING METAPHYSICAL WILL.

"DING AN SICH", A CONCEPT INTRODUCED BY IMMANUEL KANT, YET ANOTHER PHILOSOPHER. THINGS-IN-THEMSELVES ARE OBJECTS AS THEY ARE, INDEPENDENT OF OBSERVATION. SCHOPENHAUER WAS ONE OF THE FEW TO EMBRACE THIS IDEA AND BUILD UPON IT. HE TRICKLED IT DOWN TO THE INDIVIDUAL.

THE EGO, ACCORDING TO HIM, WAS THE CONFLICT BETWEEN THE INDIVIDUAL WILL AND THE WILL OF THE WHOLE. NOW THERE ARE TWO TYPES OF BEHAVIOURS. THOSE THAT AFFIRM THE WILL; AND THOSE THAT DENY IT.

THESE, I BELIEVE, COULD BE SEEN AS PLEASURE AND PAIN AS WELL.

AND THIS IS WHERE WE COME BACK TO THE FORCE FROM STAR WARS.

THE KANTIAN THING-IN-ITSELF?

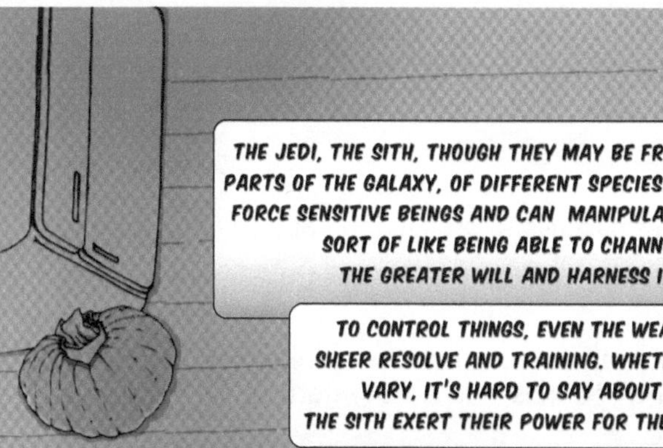

THE JEDI, THE SITH, THOUGH THEY MAY BE FROM DIFFERENT PARTS OF THE GALAXY, OF DIFFERENT SPECIES; THEY ARE ALL FORCE SENSITIVE BEINGS AND CAN MANIPULATE THE FORCE. SORT OF LIKE BEING ABLE TO CHANNELIZE THE GREATER WILL AND HARNESS IT...
TO CONTROL THINGS, EVEN THE WEAK-WILLED, BY SHEER RESOLVE AND TRAINING. WHETHER THEIR MEANS VARY, IT'S HARD TO SAY ABOUT THEIR ENDS. THE SITH EXERT THEIR POWER FOR THE SAKE OF ORDER...
YES, THEY DO THAT, THE SITH, IT'S REALLY MESSED UP HOW THEY ABUSE THEIR POWER
AND SO THEY DO, SON. BUT IF YOU REALLY THINK ABOUT SCHOPENHAUER'S PREMISE ABOUT THE EGO AND BEHAVIOURS THAT AFFIRM THE WILL AND THOSE THAT DENY IT: PLEASURE AND PAIN. YOU'LL SEE THAT IT'S THE JEDI WITH THEIR CHERISHED ASCETICISM AND CONTEMPLATION SQUANDERING THEIR GIFTS.
BUT THE JEDI... I THOUGHT... I... I NEVER REALIZED THERE WAS SO MUCH GOING ON, DOC, I WAS JUST CAUGHT UP IN THE LIGHT-SABRE BADASSERY.
INDEED THERE WAS...
AND GEORGE SAID: LET THERE BE INDUSTRIAL LIGHT & MAGIC.

#AsianFixation   **Follow** • • •

We celebrated William's successful prosecution at Benihana today. It was good cos it felt normal again.

Sheesh!

We've been together barely a month and we already sound like a suburban couple with three kids and a dog, getting by from one date night to another.

He spoke a little of his family while the sushi-chef was doing the freak show. Being a product of the one-child policy, he said he envied me for having siblings. He makes everything sound so theoretical!!! But I'd be happy to switch places with him anytime. That way, you don't have to share your parents or your stuff. And no one ever replaces you as the baby.

I guess the trial was still on his mind because he suddenly began speaking of the Chief Administrator's brilliance in bringing in the thief's sister to force a confession. JESUS!!! He called it Myoshu. Some sort of an inspired move in Go, which is some sort of Asian Chess. Must be a big deal, cos even the sushi-chef knew about it. And then they got into an argument about who invented the game, the Chinese or the Japanese. *facepalm*. Like it matters!

My silly Billy, he's so full of the far-east stuff. I hope we Americans don't sound like this to the rest of the world.

Just to get him to shut up about Big Chief, I told him I used to have a crush on that Douchebag Dandy, as he'd once called him. He reddened a little, ate his Sashimi in silence for a while and jokingly said that he now felt the same way.

I was like Whaaa? I tried telling Billy how it was SO not cool to bring in the defendant's sister like that. It's not like she did anything wrong. And what if the man was innocent? How was he going to explain it to her later on?

She reminded me so much of Tammy... all bossy like.

And then William totally tripped me up with a question—Would I feel the same way if I were Mrs Katzoff? Or her son? And then he went off on a rant about the weight of a crown, and precedents and what not. I don't remember much else, I just tuned him out.

So yea, date-night didn't go as well as I'd hoped.

But the sex was good.

Maybe I should wake him up for seconds.

15 DAYS AGO

25

We, The Children of Diablo

"When I say mutant, you say earthling!"

"Mutant..." the rapping earthling on the dais gives it up for love.

And the children, all seated with their parents, rejoin, "Earthling!!!" their hands outstretched.

"Mutant!"

"Earthling!!"

"Mutant!"

"Earthling!!"

"We live in the wasteland, we barely civilized,

Look under the skin, yo, there ain't no divide..."

The walls of the convention centre display the artwork and other projects done by the children during the course of the camp, the mosaic artfully crafted to accentuate the larger fractal. All eyes, however, stare fixedly at the boy owning the dais.

"Now I say survivor, you say earthling!"

"Survivor..." the rapping earthling prompts.

"Earthling!!" The children echo back.

"Survivor!"

"Earthling!!"

"You run on your hamster wheels,

Ooh la la, la la la, la di dah di,

Setting places on the table,

Just your plate mighty fancy."

Kilia stands in the aisle, capturing the event on her iPad, amused by the mild shock on the faces of some of the parents.

"Black, Brown, Yellow, or White,

It don't matter to Petey, that dude colour blind,

The juice in our veins, yo,

It flows monochromatic,

Same as with them animals, but oh don't you panic,

Chuck, Roast, Brisket, or Hind,

When yo mama serve em veggies, all I say is never mind!"

The boy's parents, struggling to make ends meet ever since the apocalypse, their resentment towards their destiny being replaced by a mistrust of the administration over time, feel nothing but joy and pride upon seeing their son with the Head Counsellor by his side and the Chief Administrator seated behind them in quiet dignity.

"But we all gotta eat, yo, even plants have their sap!

Feel this rap!

Step outta the gap trap!

It's almost time to clap...

So I say Mutant, you say..."

"Earthling!!" Now many of the parents join in enthusiastically as well.

"And I say Survivor, you say..."

"Earthling!!"

"Work with me now, the mission just got real!

There's a lot to be done, yo, this world's gotta heal..."

The rapping tween extends the microphone in his hand as if to drop it. But his true nature prevents him from ending on white noise. He stands there.

Earthling, indomitable.

"And that was our spoken word artist doing his flow," the Head Counsellor says over the applause and cheering from the parents in the audience as the Chief Administrator reaches across from his seat to lovingly ruffle the boy's hair.

After waiting for the ovation to end, the Head Counsellor addresses the tweens for the last time, "Congratulations, children, you are about to become full citizens. Three months ago, when you came to our little camp, there was much you didn't know. But you've all come a long way since. Learning, understanding, growing."

"We gave you our very best psychological tools, tests, exercises, shared the exemplary and inspiring work done by the likes of Mother Teresa, Chip Zullinger, Pierre Dulaine— to name a few. And in your last week here, you were given glimpses of a century and half of human history, starting with the empires, the wars, that decade of hope... the 60s, and the booms, bubbles and the crashes. Things may seem shiny and happy to you now, children, but you will face bitter truths starting tomorrow when you untainted survivors will venture out into the quarantine zone for the first time and you mutated ones will resume your lives there. That's when," she adds, "the mission will truly get real."

"But this feeling you have in your hearts right now, at this moment. Hold on to it firmly. That spirit must live on in our hearts forever. And know that if all goes well, then within your lifetime itself the domes and walls will be torn down and our planet will be Eden once again. With that, I'd like to commence this graduation ceremony of the twenty second class."

The Chief Administrator who had so far been a silent figure rises from his chair on the dais and the children, having rehearsed this several times, all follow suit.

After ensuring that they're all holding their right hand on their heart, the oath they're about to take at the ready, Josh motions for them to begin.

"We, the children of Diablo, do hereby declare," the tweens start in unison, as the Chief Administrator silently but resolutely mouths the words. "On oath, that we will absolutely and entirely renounce any and all allegiance that we may have had, to any state or sovereignty, group or individual; that we will abide by, support and defend the UN charter and the laws therein; that we will bear true faith and allegiance to the same; that we will perform non-combatant service in the peacekeeping forces when called upon by the administration; that we will perform work of importance to the administration under civilian direction when required; and that we take this obligation freely, without any agenda, reservation or purpose of evasion; we pledge ourselves to this mission—mankind's return from extinction—untainted human and mutant alike. One species indivisible. So help us God."

"Good afternoon, children," the Chief Administrator begins his address to the newly inducted child-members. "On behalf of the administration, in my capacity as the mission director for Eden (925), I welcome you as active participants to our cause."

"As you've just heard, dear Children of Diablo, our journey is going to be long. One that will require perseverance and selflessness from each and every one of us, all the way through to the end. There may be times when things may not seem fair or right but we, both untainted survivors and mutated humans alike," improvising, he adds, "Earthlings, if I may, must place our trust in the UN's reason, adhere to its charter, and abide by all directives and guidelines to stay true to the plan. You will learn about them in the months to come but the one thing you need to bear in mind right away is that you must withhold the horrible truth from all of our younger citizens."

Pausing as he registers the goose-bumps he feels, the Chief Administrator resumes, "I'm sure it must have been very hard on you when you first learnt of the apocalypse but you needed to know then. That knowledge would have been much harder to cope with later on. Any sooner, the damage would have been irreparable. You were counselled by specially trained professionals in a conducive environment— yet another example of the UN's wisdom. Never forget, my dear children, we belong to the administration."

Feeling the urge to reach for his pen, the Chief Administrator feels the essence of the oath he had made and heard innumerable times before and speaks, instead, with hand over heart. "It is an honour to serve the greatest organization in the world and a privilege to welcome you to the same."

"We, the citizens of Eden, (925)," the children begin in unison again, seeing Josh's hand on his heart and following suit, "do hereby swear that we will not let those deemed unready to learn of the apocalypse. Unwittingly or otherwise. By intent malicious or otherwise. Nor by admission, submission or omission."

Already in place by the sides of the dais, Josh and Kilia wait as the Head Counsellor calls out the names of the children. And one by one they walk up to the Chief Administrator to shake his hand and have their RFID tag cards placed around their necks. By the time this simple rite of passage conducted in dignified silence comes to an end, there isn't a dry eye in the audience.

"Now for the last part of today's graduation ceremony," the Head Counsellor says, starting to wrap things up. "The inoculation of the untainted earthlings in preparation for their first visit to the Quarantine Zone tomorrow."

As the mutated children, led by Josh, begin lining up on the dais, she continues, "While we wait for them to return, the mutated earthlings from the twenty-second class will perform the farewell song from The Sound of Music."

Kilia, having begun ushering the untainted kids towards the exit, feels a little hand grab hers and looks down to see Poo give her the puppy eyes. "We've been over this, sweetie," Kilia whispers.

"But that's my song..."

"And afterwards," the Head Counsellor adds, "I'd like all the mutated earthlings to introduce their parents to the families they stayed with for the duration of the camp. I'm sure you have lots of stories to tell."

"Before the young 'uns skedaddle, could I say something?" Mr Cooper's voice rings out from the back. "I won't take too long."

"As y'all can see," he begins a little awkwardly as soon as he's on the dais. "I'm an untainted. I was brought in from Texas to oversee the pig-farms out in the Quarantine Zone." Pausing to wipe a tear from his eye a little self-consciously, he mutters. "I've got something in my eye." And continuing as best as he can, he attempts to recover with, "I work with animals every day... And my farmhands are mostly mutants... Truth is, till my son came here, till we had a mutant child stay over, I never saw them as equals..." His face contorting with emotion again, he admits. "I remember taking this same oath with my old lady when we arrived, but it's only now... I was wrong in wanting to protect Junior from all this..."

As the Chief Counsellor puts an arm around Mr. Cooper's shoulder, he looks up and smiling through his tears continues, "Those UN shrinks, I reckon they learnt something in them fancy colleges after all."

"Thank you for sharing, Mr Cooper," the Head Counsellor says. "And what a breakthrough that was."

"A round of applause for Mr Cooper, everyone," the Chief Administrator adds, stepping forward to shake his hand.

"Sir, I'd like to apologize for the fuss we made earlier; the Lord knows I was wrong about you," Mr. Cooper says, as he hugs the Chief Administrator awkwardly and whispers in his ear, "Thank you for the bang-up job all of you in the administration are doing."

"Water under the bridge, Mr Cooper, water under the bridge," the Chief Administrator replies. Extricating himself as gracefully as he can and quickly steps off the dais.

On his way out, with Paige in tow, he instructs, "Find out what that redneck was going on about, something about a fuss he made earlier. Send flowers and a box of fine chocolates to the Head Counsellor. Best damn graduation ceremony so far— she's earned it. Let me know when she has received them so I can call to thank her myself. And that girl, the one who was making a recording at the beginning. Get me a copy of that video. Rolfe will be thrilled."

14 DAYS AGO

26

In the front row, with popcorn

The bus driver glances at the clock on the dashboard and notes, with satisfaction, that they've made good time. Just watching these teary good-byes once every three months breaks his heart and he wonders how the Counsellors do their job, day after day, camp after camp.

As he makes the turn into the crowded marketplace, slowing the bus down and darting a quick glance at the mirrors, his eyes sweep across the two peacekeepers sitting complacently in the back. Their job escorting the tweens in pairs – hand in hand to the doorstep of the mutant child's home – done, their presence in the steel reinforced bus is now perfunctory.

While Josh, all fifteen kids gathered around him, stands in the middle of the bus giving a guided tour of sorts, Kilia sits daydreaming not too far from the bus driver.

"How can they live like this!" the Cooper kid explodes. He had been agitated from the time the mutant tween who painted in black had been dropped off at the field of mud and tattered tents. And Poo, switching seats to sit next to him, had been patting his back ever since. "It's okay, Junior," she says softly. "All refugee camps look like this." The others, seeing the Quarantine Zone for the first time, are affected as well. Some near tears, a few weeping. But Josh sticks to the script. Doing his best to keep them distracted by pointing out the various sights and describing the different sounds of life in the Quarantine Zone.

"That, kids, is a Seventh Day Adventist Church. The last house of God still standing in Diablo Valley, or at least that's what Pastor Felipe would have us believe," Josh says, as the bus snakes through the crowded marketplace. "Mutated humans of all denominations and faiths go there to pray. See kids, when we lose our way in the new world we usually turn to counselling, prescribed medication or holistic therapy. But there are many who still hold on to the old ways and seek salvation in a higher power." Seeing the cross on the spire, the Cooper kid begins a 'Hail Mary,' angry tears welling in his eyes.

"These are the various factories and production units that operate here, kids," Josh explains, as they enter the industrial area of the quarantine zone after a while. "Many mutants have jobs here. They must all be at work right now, which is probably why the place is deserted. I'm sure some of your buddies' parents must be in there. Someday, your buddies may find a career here as well. If you opt for peacekeeper training you might even get to meet them every day."

As the bus driver makes a tight corner, a group of mutants, their faces masked, golden rods and flaming bottles in hand, come into view.

Kilia, still daydreaming, doesn't notice but the driver turns over his shoulder and calls out, "Peacekeepers! Looks like trouble... Shit! They've got fire-bombs. Guys!!" he calls out again, in panic.

In the blink of an eye, the bus is covered with napalm.

And though the Molotov cocktails have no effect on the steel frames and bullet-proof glass, the napalm clings to the windshield reducing the visibility to near-zero. The driver is forced to bring the bus to a screeching halt and the peacekeepers jump to their feet but do little else. One stands frozen in shock as the other screams, "Get away from the glass!"

Within seconds, the glass door, the only part of the bus that isn't welded shut, begins to crack. It is pried open soon and the attackers jump in.

The first three to make their way in focus on neutralizing the peacekeepers whose rubber batons pose no threat to their rods. The others start grabbing Kilia and the children. One of the assailants, the big one, pushes Josh aside and says gruffly, "Brother, we're doing this for you as well. Stay down!"

In a moment of clarity, Josh realizes what's really going on and the beast that lies within, the monster he's spent his whole life taming with quietude and a detached curiosity comes to the fore. Lunging towards the three attackers still working the peacekeepers, he lets himself loose. It doesn't take long before he's knocked them out and is helping the peacekeepers to their feet as he growls, "Help me save the children."

By now, the kids—all of them in shock, most of them wailing; are being bundled out. Kilia is nowhere to be seen.

With Josh leading the resurgent peacekeepers, their training finally kicking in, they begin picking off the kidnappers fighting their way out of the flaming bus and manage to push some of the children back in.

The advantage of surprise lost, the burden of struggling children weighing the abductors down, the kidnapping starts falling apart. "You!" Josh growls at one of the peacekeepers grappling with a kidnapper on the street. "Get back inside. We'll send the kids your way!" he orders, pulling the assailant away and disposing him with one powerful blow.

It isn't long before Josh and the remaining peacekeeper have most of the kidnappers lying crumpled on the street and all of the children back on the bus. Rushing back in, he does a quick headcount. Once sure that all the children are accounted for, he backs up in the bus and rushes towards the still flaming windshield with all his might.

As he slams onto the windshield, it cracks, but remains stubbornly in place. He then delivers punch after blood-stained punch until the windshield falls off the metallic frame entirely, bit by bit. Oblivious to the flaming shards lodged in his hands, Josh turns to the bus driver who had been transfixed the whole time and is now staring at him with utter disbelief. "Drive!" Facing the two peacekeepers, he adds, "I'll go after the Counsellor. You get the kids back to the Terrarium."

Turning back to the still immobilized driver, he growls, "You! I said drive!"

As the bus starts moving forward, Josh leaps out of the open doorway with a roar and chases after the last of the attackers on all fours in an animal-like parkour. Intimidated by this spectacle, the big-one drops his rod and scurries away in panic as the remaining two continue dragging Kilia away.

Seeing Josh approach, one of the remaining two attackers steps forward, twirling his golden rod with practiced ease, his knees bent and his free hand extended backwards for balance.

Lunging at the attacker with a snarl, Josh feels the rod slash through his ribcage.

Grunting with pain, but the momentum still keeping him going, he pins the attacker down. The attacker lands a second solid blow with a vertical thrust, this time on Josh's sternum causing him to lose his grip. The attacker starts to squirm away but groping wildly, Josh yanks his mask off.

"Aiko! You?!"

"Puppet!" she screeches. "You stupid, stupid puppet," she adds, struggling to her feet. But Kilia's screams bring Josh back to the moment.

One vengeful swipe from Josh is all it takes to lift Aiko off the ground sending her flying all the way to the walls of one of the factories. The sound of her skull making contact with the hard cement breaks the last attacker's will. Pushing Kilia towards Josh, he turns around and makes a run for it.

After looking about to make sure they're by themselves, the adrenaline still coursing through his veins, Josh helps her to her feet and asks, "Are you okay?"

"I... I don't know... I think I'm fine," she gasps. Her breathing is uneven and there are a few bruises on her arms and neck but she is more rattled than injured. "The children?"

"We managed to get them all, and the peacekeepers rushed them back. They'll make it fine, I think, but I don't know what we're going to do about you."

Kilia looks at the blood drain from Josh's bullet-proof shard encrusted fists and starts losing her composure when Josh steadies her with, "They may regroup and return in greater numbers. I won't be able to hold them off by myself." They stand there, holding each other upright without a touch, still coming to terms with all that's happened in mere minutes.

"We need to get you out of here, but we can't even head to the Terrarium that way," Josh says, pointing in the direction the bus headed off, knowing he's doing the thinking for the both of them. "That's what they'll expect us to do and get us somewhere along the way... SHIT!!"

"Okay!!" Kilia finally rejoins. "So we need to hide and plan a route back to the Terrarium."

Just then, a lone mutant on a bicycle emerges from one of the factories and pedals towards them, drawn by the spectacle of Aiko and her accomplices lying lifeless and chunks of napalm covered windshield still blazing on the kerb. "What happened here?" he asks but doesn't take too long to discern the incongruity in Kilia's attire. "You... You're an untainted survivor. What are you doing here? What happened?"

His instinct taking over again, Josh bristles with rage, "You tell anyone about what you've seen here, and I will..." but abruptly changing tack, he adds in a somewhat softer tone, "How about a trade? Take her gabardine hoodie, give us your coat and cap."

"What?" the mutant responds, but quickly calculating that he's getting a good deal, he removes his tattered rags and hands them over.

Kilia holds the filth she's being made to wear with disgust. Barely has she got them on that Josh begins to smear some of the limestone dust from the street onto her face and hands. "Eww..." she protests.

"There, that'll do," he says impassively, stepping back to inspect his handiwork.

27

A night. In the Zone.

"Where are we going, Josh?" Kilia asks as they backtrack their way to the marketplace. "Is there another way to the Terrarium?"

"I don't know where we're going and what we'll do once we get there," he replies in frustration. "Right now, I just want us to keep moving."

"But I have to get back to the Terrarium!" Kilia exclaims, stopping mid-step. "The inoculation's integrity degrades after twelve hours..."

"And you don't have a Haz-Mat suit on, I know," he replies, coming to a halt himself and turns to face her. "But you have to understand, the whole attack was planned well. They knew our route, the day, even the time we'd be here."

His thoughts flash to Aiko, Viktor's death, meeting them the first time at Dr Hudson's, the conversation they were having about 'the Play', the 'front row' seats the doctor had promised him.

"Josh!!"

"We still have about eleven and three quarter hours on our side," he replies, now thinking quickly. "But so do they. They must have counted on that very time-limit to pressurize the administration into getting whatever it was they were after. Fifteen children and a counsellor would have been a winning hand, but even you alone would give them leverage. They won't stop till the clock runs out. We need to find someplace to lie low until dark. Then I can take you to a location that not even Dr Hudson can pinpoint. And we'll head back early tomorrow morning. A little overexposure is a risk we'll just have to take, trust me."

"Not even Dr Hudson?" Kilia begins, puzzled. "But didn't you say he's the only family you have..."

"He knows it exists, he just doesn't know where it is," Josh interrupts brusquely. "And that's where we're going."

"Just keep up with me," he instructs, taking her hand. "Say nothing. Don't look at anyone or anything for too long." Exasperation on her face, reluctance in her steps, Kilia begins to walk. After a few steps at a quicker pace, he puts his arm lightly over her shoulder.

As they continue walking, they pass by the places Josh had been showing the kids before and eventually they're back in the marketplace. Relaxing, just a little, in the anonymity afforded by the hustle and bustle, Josh briefs Kilia in a terse whisper. "You see that corner over there? There's a basement below where we'll spend the night. But until then, we're going to take cover in the church here. This is rush hour for them, so we should be fine. Again, say nothing, but if someone smiles, try to smile back."

"Smile? I can't believe I even made it this far..." Kilia hisses, still shaken to the marrow at the thought of staying out in the Quarantine Zone for so long. "I'm dealing with post-traumatic stress here," she adds, raising one hand to show the tremor.

"Fine, just nod then and don't worry about the jitters. They'll help you blend in."

They cross the street and step up to the falafel vendor by the entrance of the church. Instead of the usual one man, they find Pastor Felipe's trio—the blind one gabbing away with the regulars blissfully, leaving the other two to do all the work. "Hey, it's Joshie!" the deaf one says when they make it to the front of the line. "Five rolls today, playa?" the blind one asks as Josh swipes his card to make the mandatory donation, adding, "Daddy's gonna get some sugar tonight!"

"Nothing gets by you, does it?" Josh replies with a forced laugh and turns to the dumb one. "Brother, do you know where the pastor is?"

"In the hall behind the sanctorum," the deaf one replies after the question is signed to him.

Making their way there, Josh and Kilia find the pastor behind a mountain of paperwork. The scowl on his face is replaced by a smile the moment he looks up. "Paying heed to my words, I see," he beams.

"No, no, it's not like that," Josh protests, but seeing the indulgent smile on the pastor's face grow wider, he decides to just go with it. "Alright Pastor, you got me! So, uh... We need to have a little quiet time... Would it be possible to... We won't get in anyone's way..."

"I'm sure you won't, son," the Pastor smiles with bliss. "Take your friend to the chapel; you know where it is, right?"

"Yes, Pastor," Josh replies both grateful and embarrassed. "Of course, Pastor..."

"Just remember, this is the Lord's home. No funny business."

Well after nightfall, when the church has emptied out, Josh and Kilia step out to find the streets of the marketplace just as deserted.

As they approach the entrance to Josh's cavern, Kilia's eyes adjust in the darkness just enough to scan the entrance to the basement of the bookshop through a wide crack that extends from the side of the building to about half the foot-path. Dead roaches abound with no ants left over to make meals out of them.

"Is this the only way in," she asks, eyeing the filth. "Through this cubby-hole?"

Chicks, Josh thinks to himself smiling inwardly but, well aware of the need to move quickly, answers with a terse, "Yes. Follow me," and crawls down into the darkness.

The first thing Kilia sees as the oil lamps flicker to life are Josh's eyes. Iridescent in the orange filter glow of the room, his pupils contracting in a cat-like manner. Feeling her heart skip a beat, she averts her gaze.

"Why don't we sit over there," Josh says, stumbling back self-consciously, as he motions to one corner.

Settling down on one of the mahogany chairs by the hardwood table, Kilia takes in the cramped room—books of all shapes and sizes on wall to wall shelves, an assortment of tools, glues and tapes on the table between them and a small doorway in one corner.

"I love what you've done with the place," she teases.

"Oh no, I found it like this." Josh owns up right away. Never having had a brush with this shade of Kilia. "Everything you see in here except the lamps was already here. When I first discovered this place late one night, chasing a rat down the hole, I used to live off the streets with..."

"With?" Kilia asks, her curiosity piqued.

"You said once that you wanted to see my cave of wonders," Josh replies after an awkward silence. "Well, here we are."

"Cave of wonders, huh?" Kilia smiles. "I didn't know you

liked to read. I read quite a bit too, but I do that on my iPad. It's convenient and everything, but I miss the feel of the pages as I turn them, the smell of ink on paper..."

"The senses deceive from time to time, and it is prudent never to trust wholly those who have deceived us even once," Josh quotes Descartes. His conflicted feelings manifest in his choice of words and his tone of voice. That it was the good doctor who shared this pearl of wisdom whilst calling it a lie only makes it worse for him.

"Nice!" Kilia exclaims. "Is that yours or did you read it in one of these books?" And rising, she steps up to one of the shelves. Walking slowly with her fingers running over the spines, she continues, "You were right to bring me here, you know. As long as we make it back safe to the terrarium, it will have been the right thing to do. I've heard about people staying out in quarantine zones for up to eighteen hours and being just fine."

"It's been a rough day," Josh sighs, his thoughts still lingering over his maker. "Will you be fine on the floor? I never got around to getting sheets or anything..."

"I think I'll manage. I nearly passed out when we were in the church."

"Let's get to it, then," Josh says, rising from his chair.

"But now that we're here or maybe because that drowsiness has passed, I feel like I can go on all night. Shall we read a little?" she says as she reaches for a book.

"We have a long walk ahead of us tomorrow, Kilia. When will you sleep?"

"When you put me to sleep," she replies with a coy smile. "Like you do with our kids every day at... The kids!" Her smile gone, Kilia starts to hyperventilate. "I hope they're alright. They must be so traumatised... I'm sure their parents will need therapy after this as well... My parents! I can't even begin to imagine what they must be going through..."

"Kilia..." Josh stands facing her, his hands on her shoulders. "Please lie down and close your eyes, I'll talk you through it."

"Your toes are relaxing," Josh starts off in a soothing tone. "The soles of your feet are relaxing. Feel your feet relaxing..." Methodically working his way up until he reaches the top of her head verbally with the Shava-asana, he waits for her breathing to slow down. And after seeing her breathing pattern change, knowing he's done all he can, he settles down next to her for some much-needed rest.

Curling up, he feels pain shoot through his side, and reaching out to investigate, he finds blood from Aiko's gash. Apprehensive, since he doesn't want to lose his strength before he can get Kilia back safely, he uses some of the old cellophane tape that has been sitting on the table to stem the flow as best as he can.

Sometime in the middle of the night, Kilia wakes up with a start. Warm, flush and covered with sweat. But seeing Josh next to her, sleeping like a child, she tells herself that she'll be home soon enough. And after a while, she finds herself drifting off, curling up against Josh.

13 DAYS AGO

28

Josh. The Immortal.

"Wake up, Kilia, time to get going..."

Still snuggled up against Josh's warmth, she mumbles, "Go away, Djane..."

"Kilia!" He gives her a gentle shake. "You've been out in the Quarantine Zone for nearly ten hours now!"

Kilia sits up with a start, the events of the previous day flashing before her eyes.

Emerging from the basement, they cross the empty lots and soon stand before the wooden fence that lines the hills. "Now what?" she asks, discouraged by the insurmountable obstacle.

"Grab my shoulders, hop on my back, and straddle my waist."

Springing to action the moment she is in position, Josh scales the fence quickly and gracefully dismounts on the other side with Kilia still holding on. The pain shoots through his side as he lands. Making its way from his chest, going all the way down to his knee, but Josh bites it back wordlessly and begins ascending the sheer rock face of the mountain.

As they're working their way up, the skies start to lighten and Kilia witnesses the radioactive dust clouds painted by the rising sun, something she's never seen before. Lost in the beauty of it all, she's jolted back to reality when Josh loses his grip on one of the rocks.

"Are you sure you can take me all the way up? Do you think I might be able to climb myself?"

"I'll manage," Josh wheezes. "And don't worry, there are some trails in the middle of our journey to the top that you'll be able to walk on. I'll recover there enough to carry you the rest of the way."

Once they're up the mountain, Josh lowers himself to let her dismount. She steps to the edge, taking in the view the peak affords as Josh slowly rises to his feet, and between deep breaths he asks, "Think you'll be able to climb down by yourself?"

Peering down the precipice leading to the fields that stretch all the way to the Terrarium in the distance, Kilia isn't quite sure she can.

"You can do it," he encourages, with a smile. "I'll be right next to you all the way."

"This is safe, right?" Kilia whispers, as they make their way through the fields.

"As safe as it can be," he replies. "The farm-hands are staring only because we're strangers waltzing about this early in the day. Yesterday's attack may have been a well-planned exercise but I doubt any of these folks are involved."

"Delta One Three to all personnel," seeing them coming the wrong way through a pair of high powered binoculars, a peacekeeper manning his post raises a yellow alert. "Two mutants approaching on foot. Two clicks from perimeter, western quadrant. Shift Supervisor, please advise."

"Hold position," a voice cackles back. "Big bird in transit."

The Chief of Security arrives with his deputy in tow. Taking a second look, the Deputy Chief of Security recognizes Kilia. "I think the girl's an untainted, Chief," he says. "Probably the one abducted yesterday. Looks like the friendly brought her back," he says, handing the binoculars to his boss.

The Chief of Security, taking a look, nods in agreement, adding, "She's been out for more time than the safety protocols allow. Send out a van, have them escorted to the decontamination chambers. The friendly's limping and may need treatment."

"Shift Supervisor, this is Little Bird," the Deputy Chief of Security relays the order. "Despatch pick-up crew. Package hot, I repeat, package hot."

Seeing a van approach in the distance, the familiar shape, colours and markings, Josh feels the sheer will that kept him going so far begin to dissolve. He comes to a stop, resting all his weight on his good side.

The van pulls up soon after and two peacekeepers jump out. "Are you injured?" one of them asks while the other prattles off the orders they've been given. "We're here to escort you to the decontamination zone on the other side for the medical evaluation and treatment you need. Please get on board; there's water and emergency food rations."

"Chief Administrator's office. How may I help you?" Paige

answers.

"We can't say for sure yet but it looks like the girl from yesterday has returned, brought back by a friendly. I have orders to convey this to the Chief Administrator myself."

"Please hold!"

Less than a minute later, Paige is summoned into the Chief Administrator's office. As she walks in, she can't help but notice the smile returning to his face. Despite everything, he had managed to remain poised throughout. But it's the fatigue now creeping through the smile that reveals the effort the Chief Administrator had expended in order to stay composed. No. 2 is utterly relieved and makes no bones about it, with the look of a man who survived a car crash without as much as a scratch.

"Miss Paige, time for another update to Rolfe," the Chief Administrator instructs right away. "But first, I need you to find William."

By the time Josh and Kilia arrive at the decontamination chambers, they find a battery of biogenetic engineers, technicians and medical personnel ready and waiting.

Standing on the conveyor belt, knowing he has done all he can for her, Josh finally gives in to the pain. Clutching the bandaged, yet bleeding wound, he counts second after painful second until the blowers are done drying him. The very last of his strength expended, he collapses onto the stretcher that awaits.

Shocked to see Josh being wheeled away as she steps out of the decontamination chambers, Kilia grabs the technician pushing the back of the stretcher. "What happened? Where are you taking him?"

"Let go!" she snaps, shaking Kilia's hand off, still carting Josh away. "He needs a transfusion. And a glucose feed. Stat!"

"Josh!" she trails along, "Josh…"

As the stretcher is carted through the exit, the peacekeeper standing guard at the doorway blocks her. "You can't go any further, Miss."

"But…"

"They'll do their best for him Kilia, just let them get to it." Hearing the well-known voice from over her shoulder, she turns to see the Deputy Chief Administrator standing with someone vaguely familiar. "Why don't we find someplace quiet where we can talk?" No. 2 continues, gently taking her by the hand.

Once they're seated, William takes the lead, "Miss Bagyoko, could you tell us what happened after the bus left you and your co-counsellor behind?"

"He came and rescued me…" Kilia begins narrating, staring at the exit Josh was carted through. "He fought off the attackers, took me back to the marketplace…" She pauses, reliving the trauma, "There, we took shelter in a church."

"The one run by Pastor Felipe?" William interjects, a little incredulously.

"Yes. And then we spent the night in the basement of what must have been an old bookshop. Early this morning, we set out on foot across the fields to return. I didn't realize he was hurt. Will he be ok?"

"Alright, Kilia, that's good enough for now," No. 2 says, rising. "We have to restrict you to isolation chambers for testing and observation. Standard procedure, you see. Just follow the biogenetic engineers waiting over there. William will keep you company. And oh," he adds, "I'm going over to meet your parents, give them the good news. Anything you'd like to say?"

#ThereSheIs   **Follow** • • •

I was hoping to take off early yesterday to doll up for the upcoming day of rest, which is today btw, when the report of the attack on the bus came in. Obviously there was no way to get out of the cluster-fuck the administrative office turned into.

The Chief Administrator stayed over. As did No. 2 and William. And even though there was nothing any of us little people could do, we all stayed put until No. 2 went from desk to desk telling us to go get some rest.

As I was passing by the security section to get the Chief Administrator a snack, I noticed their Chief totes off-the-hook. There were maps with pins on the wall, wireless reports coming in, a full-scale search and rescue operation raging.

The peacekeepers had it the worst I guess. And those two, the ones who were on the bus with the kids, I really hope Rambo lets them out of the stockade now.

And Chief Big-talk... From the report he just had me tap out to Rolfe, he made it sound like he Liam Neesoned her back with his very particular set of skills... Ugh!

I hope they let Will go soon.

♡ ⇄

29

Parthe-Neon-Genesis

Decked in full bio-hazard armour, two of Dr DeChampeaux's technicians stand behind a protective lead curtain. All contact, despite all the precautions at this stage, is made via robotic arms.

The first check is for radiation levels and gamma ray residue. Pleasantly surprised, the two technicians exchange nods and turn to the camera that gives Kilia a view of their side of the room. "Congratulations," the first technician says, "you're not radioactive."

The gravity of her own situation eclipsed by her concern for Josh, all she can manage is a nod.

The threat of contamination dismissed, the second technician pushes a button on the console and the robotic arms retract into the overhanging case, while the lead curtains slide back into the sides of the evaluation chamber. "We'll start by collecting blood, urine and stool samples," the first technician says, approaching. "You can use the restroom in the back for the urine and stool right after we finish drawing blood," as he proceeds to tighten a strap below Kilia's bicep.

Numb to the needle prick, she awakens from her reverie as the technician labels the vacutainer 'Subject 2'.

"The mutant who brought me back to the Terrarium," she asks, "is he alright now?"

"Miss," the second technician who had been busying himself wiping down the containers for the urine and stool answers, "I'm sure the doctors are doing their best. Why don't we make sure that you're good too? Here," he continues, as he hands her the plastic cups, "and there," he adds, pointing Kilia in the right direction.

As the technicians wait for Kilia to return, the second turns to the first, "So you're Dr DeChampeaux's favourite eh? Now that your theory on the stolen Styrofoam got validated by empirical data."

"You know how temperamental she can be," the first replies with a smug smile. "And whose blowpipe did you have to rinse to land this job of collecting stool samples?" The second shrugs the jibe off with a laugh, but the first technician is just getting warmed up. "You take shit from everyone you meet day after day, eh?"

Placing the samples on a tray once Kilia has returned, the second technician puts on surgical gloves and takes a saliva swab as well. As he steps out with the tray, the first technician announces, "And for my next trick, the CT Scan."

Helping her on the examination table, he instructs, "It won't take too long but please don't move your head. If you do, we'll have to start over." As the scanner buzzes to life, Kilia, an agnostic for most of her adult life, finds herself praying for Josh. "Truly distress has seized me, but Thou art the most merciful of those that are merciful... Remove the harm, O Lord of humankind and heal him, for You are the healer and there is no healing except Your healing, with a healing which does not leave any disease behind..."

"Miss, we need to check for marks, rashes or pigmentation," the second technician says after the scan. "A nurse is here, waiting to carry out a full visual, an orifice check and administer a hearing and vision test."

"Could you excuse us," the first technician adds, "while we slip into something more comfortable?"

"Two atoms are walking down the street," the first technician says. "The first atom tells the second, 'I think I lost an electron.' So the second atom asks, 'Are you positive?'" Outfitted in lab coats now, the technicians kill time with William. And his will to live.

"No matter how many times I hear that joke, it never gets old," the second technician guffaws good naturedly. "Tough crowd, eh?" he adds, noting the grimace on William's face.

How about something Stephen Wright-ish then?" the first technician persists. "Do radioactive cats have 18 half-lives?" Vaguely remembering the Reddit thread on this one-liner, but putting on the brightest smile he can manage to bring his suffering to an end, William replies, "Epic, man, that's just epic!"

"She has 20-20 vision," the nurse declares matter of factly, as the door behind her closes. "Her hearing is well above average and everything else is the way it should be—we're good here," she concludes and marches off.

"Don't forget us when you're in high places, bro-heim," the first technician bids William a breezy farewell. "We should head back and report to Dr DeChampeaux," the second technician adds, following the first one out.

Now left to himself, William wonders how he's going to break the news.

After considering having a word with Paige but deciding against it, he steps into the evaluation chamber with a sense of dread. Facing Kilia, hand extended, he awkwardly begins, "I'm William... we met earlier? I'll take any details you might want to add to your statement, answer questions..."

Rising to shake the proffered hand, Kilia responds with a smile, "The Administrative Associate, I remember now, from the trial. You're here to babysit me, aren't you?" As William nods in acknowledgement, she wipes the tense smile off his face with, "Any word on Josh?"

"Perhaps we should sit down."

"So..." Not getting an answer even after they're seated, Kilia repeats emphatically, "How is he?" William looks at his feet for a moment, then back at Kilia, dead in the eye. "He didn't make it. But your parents are overjoyed that you're safe," he adds quickly, as she sits in a stunned silence.

An eternity passes by but Kilia remains saturnine. "He had lost a lot of blood..." William fumbles, never before at such a loss of words. "His unique mutation... The transfusion was rejected. The doctors did all they could..." Wondering if his words are getting through, he continues just the same. "He died a hero, Kilia. He was instrumental in protecting the children, he brought you back safely as well... He didn't suffer either."

"And the children?"

A hopeful smile dawns on William's face as he answers, "They're all fine. They made it back safe. They're a little traumatized, but you, their counsellor, would be the best person to ease them over that difficult experience. As soon as you get the final all clear yourself, of course."

A lone teardrop streaks its way down her cheek as she sits there wordlessly, crushed by the realization that she will never see Josh again.

"And as I was saying, your parents are really thankful to have you back," William continues, still trying.

"My parents..." Kilia echoes blankly. "They're thankful."

"Yes, they are!" William starts emphatically but unwilling to upset her inadvertently, he stops.

Just then, the two technicians return, accompanied by their supervisor, the nurse in tow. "We need to get one more test done, miss. Mr Saturday Night here didn't catch the anomalies in your urine," the second technician gripes. "I could say the same about you, Hoser!" the first one spits back.

"I've had it with you two!" the nurse, her patience worn thin, sternly commands. "Take it outside!"

"Kilia..." William says softly, realizing she isn't moving a muscle. "Just one more and we can call it a day, come on," and he leads her to the examination table. The nurse has her move her upper garment all the way up to her sternum and applies gel to her stomach and abdominal areas as the senior technician wheels the ultrasound machine over.

Transducer in hand, his eyes fixed on the monitor, the technician scans Kilia's abdomen, making a recording of his report. "Nothing out of the ordinary with the kidneys. Stomach seems fine, small intestine, large intestine good too." Slowing down a little he adds, "The uterus seems extended. Tumour maybe?"

Seeing the nurse shrug ambivalently, he instructs, "You want to send in the clowns?"

"I don't know, sir. I just take the shit around here," the second technician remarks acridly, back in the room and not even bothering to look at the monitor. "Could we look deeper?" the first technician asks. "I thought I saw it pulsing." After tilting the transducer one way and then another, the senior technician turns to the first, "Good call!" Turning to Kilia, he adds, "Congratulations, you're pregnant."

"What?!" Kilia exclaims, sitting up on the table.

"That, over there is a month-old foetus," the first technician says, pointing to the screen. "And by the looks of it, seems quite healthy too." "Congratulations, miss," the second technician adds.

"But that's not possible. I'm a virgin!"

The nurse, after taking a look at Kilia's intact hymen a second time, heads out of the room to find the technicians and William awaiting her with bated breath.

"She's not lying."

"Parthenogenesis!" the first technician exults.

"It's a type of asexual reproduction in which the offspring develops from unfertilized eggs," the senior technician responds to William's silent question. "Quite common among lower life forms, also found in some species of fish, birds and reptiles. Never before seen in mammals."

"Not if you count the immaculate conception," the first technician snarks, high-fiving the second.

"*Tā mā de!*" William swears. "Where's the nearest communication booth?"

12 DAYS AGO

30

The Plague. The Mutation. The Mother.

With hints of dark circles under his eyes, the Chief Administrator sits at his desk, his thoughts racing over the events of the previous evening, starting from the time he received word of the inexplicable pregnancy as he sips his nth cup of coffee—a beverage he avoids like the plague.

Click. Click. Click.

I have awaited the Second Coming not just after the apocalypse but for as long as I can remember, the sentimental idiot had blathered before Dr DeChampeaux stormed in.

Click. Click. Click.

That insolent French bitch! Threatening to go over my head, straight to the UN Committee for the final solution. Where does she find the gall?

Click. Click. Click.

And the Chief of Medicine, that spineless bleeding heart, he actually recited the Hippocratic Oath! I swear by Apollo and everything... and then actually went on to lecture me, citing studies about foetuses sending stem cells to the mother as an immune response— implying I wasn't proposing abortion, but murder!

Click. Click. Click.

It was a mistake having all three in room at the same time.

Click. Click. Click.

And the dinner I invited Jorge to later on, what a glorious waste. I may as well have flushed the '86 Sassicaia straight down the john. The more he drank, the more devout he got. And the more devout he got, the more impatient I became.

Click. Click...

Feeling the clicker jam, the Chief Administrator takes a moment to snap it back in place.

Probably shouldn't have said, 'We don't have time for your fantasies, Jorge, just sign the damn thing.' Not only did he tear up my Executive Order and leave right away, he hasn't said a word to me since.

Stepping into the isolation chamber, his thoughts in a swirl, the Chief Administrator is somewhat unprepared for the tender sight that awaits him. Kilia stands beyond the glass wall, one hand on her belly, the other on the glass. Khady stands with her hand on the glass as well, her hand across her daughter's and the other around Alasco's drooping shoulders.

"Allah has said pray to me," Alasco softly declares, his eyes downcast, "so that I may answer." He points in the direction diametrically opposite the door the Chief Administrator has gently closed behind him.

As the family offers supplications together in dignified silence, the Chief Administrator—his arrival still unnoticed— waits respectfully.

"As-salāmu Alaykum," the Chief Administrator says, just as the Bagyokos turn towards each other after the prayer.

"Wa alaykumu as-salam," the words escape Alasco's lips.

"Chief Administrator!" Khady exclaims, startled, and quickly adds, "Good day, sir."

"There's nothing good about this day, Khady," Alasco mumbles, eyes downcast again.

"Have you been here long?" the Chief Administrator asks.

"No, we just got here, sir," Khady replies.

With a sympathetic nod at Kilia, the Chief Administrator continues, "We're doing all we can for your daughter. I know the situation must be terribly frightening, but I assure you, you're in good hands."

"Could we have a word, sir?" Alasco asks humbly.

"Of course, Mr Bagyoko. This way please," the Chief Administrator replies, taking Alasco to the far corner of the observation chamber. "Yes?" he prompts, when Alasco doesn't speak even though they're out of earshot.

"Who is the father of my daughter's child?"

"Well, that's a tough one, because the doctors have confirmed that Kilia is a..." the Chief Administrator pauses to frame his answer better. "Your daughter hasn't dishonoured you."

"But that mutant boy?" Alasco continues, a little agitated. "The one she spent the night with in the Quarantine Zone?"

"I'm sorry to say that in bringing your daughter back, he lost his life. And we don't have any legitimate scientific theories about his role in... this situation. So, at this point, it's all just speculation really."

"Alasco..." Khady calls out, as a technician accompanied by a nurse enters Kilia's side of the isolation chamber in bio-hazard suits. "The doctors are here. Come, come."

They stand in silence, close to the glass wall, as the sounds of the machine filter through the speakers above. The moment the foetus comes up on the monitor, the technician starts recording his report. "2:17 p.m., Sonogram for Subject 2. The foetus has grown considerably. The child appears to be male and seems quite healthy. If its development continues at this rate, the mother will go into labour within weeks."

The technician then begins rattling off jargon that neither the Chief Administrator nor the Bagyokos understand, but the Chief Administrator has heard enough. "The doctors know what they're doing and we can let them do their jobs," he says, turning to Khady and Alasco. "I can't even begin to imagine how you must feel, but there is a way out..."

"Way out?" Alasco echoes.

"We can always terminate. I mean, this isn't what anyone wanted in the first place. So, there's no reason not to do it and as I was saying earlier, the best of our medical team is already allocated to Kilia's case."

"But that is haram!" Alasco responds emphatically.

"Yes," Khady nods, turning to look at Kilia through the glass, adding, "forbidden by our faith."

Just then, Paige steps into the isolation chamber, startling the Chief Administrator and the Bagyokos alike. "Yes, Miss Paige," the Chief Administrator says, recovering quickly. "What brings you here?"

"Your 2:30, sir. Councilman David is waiting at the office."

"Right, of course," the Chief Administrator responds. Turning back to the Bagyokos, he says, "I apologize, but I must head back," and with the most sincere expression he can manage, adds, "I respect your faith, your laws. But this here, it may not even be a child as we know it. I urge you to reconsider the only option we have."

Seeing the Chief Administrator striding towards his office,

David rises to his feet with a smile. "Good afternoon Chief, here as requested."

"Yes David, thank you," the Chief Administrator says curtly. "The situation has transformed into something else entirely but we should talk. Follow me." Turning to Paige, he adds, "Could you send in No. 2?"

Picking up his pen as he sits, the Chief Administrator begins clicking away at ten-second intervals as David tactfully waits in silence. Less than a minute has gone by before No. 2 joins them wordlessly. "Why don't you brief David on recent events," the Chief Administrator instructs, as soon as his deputy is seated.

"Yes, Chief Administrator. A bus bringing back fifteen untainted children and their counsellors from the Quarantine Zone was attacked two days ago..."

"That's when I scheduled this meeting with you, David," the Chief Administrator interjects.

"The peacekeepers, assisted by the mutant counsellor, managed to bring the children back safely. The untainted counsellor was rescued by her co-counsellor. He brought her back the next day safe and sound, but she was exposed to fallout for an extended period, you see."

"Oh, so she's showing signs of mutation, is she?" David asks.

Before No. 2 can answer, Dr DeChampeaux bursts into the Chief Administrator's office with a distraught Paige in tow. "I tried telling Dr DeChampeaux that you were busy in a meeting, sir," Paige cries. "But she just wouldn't listen."

"What can I do for you, Doctor?" the Chief Administrator asks icily.

"You can stop manipulating the girl's parents into an abortion!" the Frenchwoman huffs. "I thought I already told you how significant this child of mutation is. And in my professional opinion, must be brought into this world so that we can study and benefit from it. I could not fully support Dr Alfred Hudson's proposal for in-utero experimentation on moral grounds. But it is for those very reasons that this child must live," she rages on. "Would you like me to invite the Chief of Medicine so he can repeat his oath once again?"

"Dr DeChampeaux... please, what makes you think I would do such a thing?" the Chief Administrator asks wearily.

"Faire la une!!" She exclaims. "I heard your voice on the recording of the report. The isolation chambers have two-way microphones. They caught everything."

"Right, of course," the Chief Administrator replies, not losing composure. "Alright, doctor, you have me."

But the good doctor persists. "I'm not leaving until I have your assurance that you won't try again."

"Alright, doctor, you have my word," the Chief Administrator submits. "Now may I get back to my meeting?"

"Bien," Dr DeChampeaux says and storms out, as No. 2 crosses himself, rage brimming in his eyes.

"So where were we...?" the Chief Administrator asks.

"Child of mutation." David prompts.

"Abu, you have to believe me when I say that nothing happened that night. I did nothing I shouldn't have." Kilia looks at her parents beseechingly but seeing them unmoved, adds, "I've spent enough time with the medical staff here to know that they're just as baffled as we are."

Alasco turns away in frustration and repeats through clenched teeth, "I don't believe you."

"I swear, abu, we didn't even kiss, if that's what you're

thinking."

Balking at the thought, Alasco lets out a long and angry breath. Facing Khady, he says, "I told you to keep a closer watch on your daughter. I knew she had a soft spot for that outsider. One night and this is what happens."

"My daughter?!" Khady exclaims. "She's been the apple of your eye and now you accuse me?"

"That mutant boy, Josh," Alasco refuses to back down. "He had accelerated growth too, didn't he? And now this child in Kilia's womb is... He was the only mutant she had any interaction with during her time out there. Who else could it be?"

Her thoughts going to Josh, Kilia begins to weep.

"Stop this, Alasco," Khady reproaches. "You're making our daughter cry." Turning to Kilia, she asks, "So you swear that you did nothing..." working through her own embarrassment slowly. "And there was no contact... of any sort..."

"Yes ma..." Kilia replies through her tears.

"Alright, alright... Stop crying dear and wipe those tears away." Turning to her still agitated husband, Khady adds, "I believe her, Alasco, you should too."

"Even if I believe her," he replies, choking on his own tears, "What about the child?"

7 DAYS AGO

31

Deus-Ex-Nukina

"Technology, if sufficiently advanced, can be indistinguishable from magic," Dr Hudson begins with passion long lost, the hope it would ever return abandoned somewhere along the way. "Some of you may have heard of this so-called law proposed by Arthur C. Clarke, but even to those who haven't, the truth in these words is self-evident."

"The miracle that was bestowed upon us, on this very hallowed ground but twelve days ago," Pastor Felipe solemnly intones, not too far from the now derelict baseball field where the good doctor stands holding court, "has brought some of you back to this Church and all of you," sweeping his eyes across the multitude to give the illusion of eye contact, "each and every one of you, back to faith." Pausing once again for effect and noting the tears well up in the eyes of many new parishioners with satisfaction, he deals the coup de grace. "Welcome home."

The feed to the ubiquitous view screens in the Quarantine Zone that perpetually aired UN propaganda, had been interrupted once.

Late in the night after the peacekeepers and untainted human survivors had retreated back to the terrarium, statements by Dr Hudson and Pastor Felipe had played and the news about Kilia Bagyoko's inexplicable conception had spread through the Quarantine Zone like wildfire.

"For the longest time, mankind has balked at the thought of playing God with human cloning, genetic engineering and designer babies." Careful not to dwell on his own fall from grace, Dr Hudson presses on, "But given where we find ourselves, having done nothing to bring about the circumstances that have led to this development, hoping only to augment them at most as dictated by our inherent survival instinct, we must, with a clear conscience..."

"Bear witness!" Pastor Felipe proclaims, emboldened by the enthusiasm that is palpably spreading across the church. "As you all know, our saviour, the King of kings, the Lord of lords, was bestowed upon us at this very spot. He will be among us soon enough. As he protects his mother from this ghastly affliction, so shall he shepherd us all."

"I have to admit that at this point in time, it is difficult to say with certainty how both the mother and child show no signs of mutation or explain the anomaly even, much less determine the applications of its by-products," not wanting to lose his audience to scientific terminology, Dr Hudson skips ahead. "But this, most likely, is evolution at work. I am not here to refute this miracle, as some might call it, but rather I come to you with a desire to study it through the lens of scientific method. And after gaining an understanding of the underlying microbiology, use that knowledge to alleviate our suffering."

"Haven't we suffered enough?" Pastor Felipe chokes with more emotion than he actually feels. "I ask the Lord every day, but when I first learnt about this miracle, I knew the time of our troubles had come to an end." He pauses, sweeping the crowd with his eyes once again. "As some of you know, the Administration turned down a request to rebuild this church despite all the sacrifices we made in putting together the UN credits needed for such an endeavour. Now this hallowed ground has shown its power. Now they will not be able to stop us with their oppressive policies and regulations. But I digress; when I first learnt about the Immaculate Conception…"

"I reached out to as many as I possibly could by issuing a public statement that some may have seen," Dr Hudson continues. "The first meeting was poorly attended, but the next day was better. The day after that, there were even more, and look at us now. The road that lies ahead, I tried walking this very path alone, before. Then, I was expunged by the Administration, but now that we all stand together, they will have no choice but to make way. This first ever recorded case of parthenogenesis in a human is astounding to say the least, but all the research that I managed to get done in the past has me convinced that this as yet unborn child holds the key…"

"The door to the heavenly sanctuary is about to open, now that our Lord, the High Priest, has cleansed our sins with his blood," Pastor Felipe rhapsodizes. "His return from Orion Nebula is imminent. But we must clear every obstacle that stands in his way. He relies upon our faith, and the deeds our faith compels us to, to be brought into our world…"

"A world that is, unfortunately, still subject to the whims and fancies of the United Nations. So far, we haven't done anything concrete in dealing with the Administration to secure the child's safety," Dr Hudson continues, "but the UN delegate will be here tomorrow. And tomorrow, we must all march out and manifest our intent. And show our strength if we must."

"Stand with me, along the route from the train station to the terrarium, the time has come," Pastor Felipe thunders. "Restrain yourselves, demonstrate with grace, but be sure to play your part."

"I urge each and every one to sign the petition we've filed with the Mutant Council demanding the Administration hand Kilia Bagyoko to a newly constituted research team at the General Hospital along with the necessary tools, implements, devices and resources to carry out the research. As a man of science," Dr Hudson continues, his tone still even but unmistakably determined, "I don't have the luxury of belief, but I don't question the faith of those who see this event as the fulfilment of a prophecy coming to fruition either. Give me the chance to pursue this anomaly and I will see it through to its rightful end. You have my word."

"Now let us pray to our Lord who brings us our salvation. And let us pray for the men of science who will bring us the communion!" Pastor Felipe booms hysterically, his hands in the air, stirring the congregation to a frenzy. "The Body, The BLOOD! Of the Saviour... in their labs!"

"We end our service today with *The Carol of the Bells,*" Pastor Felipe's blind volunteer announces from the side over the din, as the choir lines up by the pulpit.

#ThankfulForTheInternet   **Follow** • • •

I surprised my Silly Billy with Penne a la Arrabiata last night. I guess the wine I'd served got him all chatty, but at least he makes sense now. Yesterday's WILLTalk was on Cultural lag—the gap between our cultural values & practices and our tech. When he told me that we'd figured out how to edit genes and clone people as far back as 1998, I was like *yawn* whatevs.

But then he made it real. Like, really real. It would be like coding and designing a person, he said, like we do for our online avatars, and then 3D printing them organically.

And I was like Whoa...

It was hard to keep up with Will over dinner, but now that I've looked it all up from the recording (I've begun recording our conversations and looking stuff up afterwards), it's really got me trippin.

Why are we so afraid of change?

Mutation is actually how evolution happens in the first place. And you gotta give it to the Dalai Lama. He's still the only leader of a world religion who's totes #ForTransHumanism.

And then Billy went off on religion. (Blew his load, is more like it) How religion is nothing but society's gamification of its morality. AND mortality. Getting to Heaven is like getting the top score? Ixxthus!!

I'm probably going to rot in hell just for blogging this. Billy ended it all on a nice note, tho. #DanteWasWrong #FrancisOfAssisiLives

Maybe I should write to Caleb about all this, he'll be able to relate. All he used to do was play DotA. Or was it Age of Empires? Or was it GTA? Dayumnnn... Rep++ yo. I think it's all coming together in my head now.

Anyhoo, too bad I can't tell him about the counsellor and the baby she's popping out of thin air. Stupid Big-Chief-Do-Nothing and his blonde gag order. Something this cray and less than 20 of us know.

6 DAYS AGO

32

Oz

"Why isn't the UN delegate coming here in a plane, Billy? Isn't he, like, super important?" Paige whispers as they wait at the train station a few miles away from the Terrarium that connects Diablo Valley to the rest of the world.

"Because planes can't be made out of lead," William whispers back, hoping none of the others standing around, especially the Chief Administrator, has overheard the exchange.

It isn't long before the radiation proof lead-lined train pulls up billowing smoke. As Rolfe steps out of the executive carriage in a bio-hazard suit, the first thing that strikes him is that while the Chief Administrator is in attendance with a mutated human and the rest of his entourage, No. 2 is nowhere to be seen.

After a "Hello everyone" to the welcoming party, Rolfe remarks, "I see you've left your deputy behind, Administrator," grasping the Chief Administrator's hand.

"Jorge has mixed feelings about the situation and I've given him some time off to get back on the horse," the Chief Administrator replies blithely. "But anyway, our transport awaits. This way..." Turning to his Administrative Associate, he adds, "Ride back with the others, I'll escort the delegate with Councilman David in the first van."

"And what is it exactly that you do for us, David?" Rolfe

begins, noting the camaraderie between Chief and Davie.

"He's a Councilman, sir," the Chief Administrator replies. "He heads the outreach program." Seeing David's polite smile met with a cold silence, he continues, "He's proven his worth to us in a considerably short period of time as our inside man out in the Quarantine Zone. And he helps with the 'fire-side chats' as well. You know, the ones I send you from time to..."

"No offence but much to our surprise, the Administrator hasn't been up to the mark lately," Rolfe interrupts sternly. Turning to face the Chief Administrator, he continues, "The Styrofoam that sprouted legs, went for a walk and came back mixed in gasoline... While we stand by the judgment delivered by the jury, the matter should have been pursued further. The mutant named by the accused... His name escapes me now..."

"Viktor!" David pipes up.

Deflating David with a scathing glance, Rolfe resumes, "Clearly his timely death should have tipped you off. And the attack on the bus should have never come to pass. What happened to the girl—it would have been impossible to foresee but be that as it may, I am here to do what you failed to accomplish."

The Chief Administrator, not used to being berated at such length and that too while others are present, replies quietly, "I'm glad you've stepped in, sir."

Seated in the conference room of the Administrative Office, Rolfe watches the statements made by Pastor Felipe and Doctor Hudson on the big screen. Everyone present has seen the video before, so when the lights come on, all eyes turn to him.

After gazing in the middle distance, the full import of how bad things could have gone if the Chief Administrator had dealt with the situation as he had been instructed still sinking in, he finally breaks the silence. "That explains the crowds of mutants that had lined up all the way from the train station to the perimeter of the terrarium."

Sensing that Rolfe wasn't going to say much else at this point in time, the Chief Administrator addresses him, "Had it not been for David's diligence, we wouldn't have managed to get our hands on this tape either."

Breaking protocol, the Chief of Security blurts, "Mr Delegate, Sir, I'm leading the investigation myself. William's helping, same as before. And it shouldn't be too long before we get our hands on the person who made and aired the tape. It may be more than one person but either way, one of them would have to have access to the broadcast system. We're interrogating everyone at the chambers of the Mutant Council and..."

"At this point," raising his hand, Rolfe silences the Chief of Security, "that is of no consequence."

"Exactly!" the Chief of the Mutant Council interjects. "You saw the people yourself, Delegate, and you should know, our offices have been inundated with requests and petitions to declare Miss Bagyoko a mutated human, move her to the Quarantine Zone immediately, and under the watchful eyes of Dr Alfred Hudson deliver the promised child."

"The promised child?" Rolfe sputters, finally showing emotion. "That's probably just the product of some sort of mutation we haven't seen so far."

"Exactly!" the Chief Councilman rejoins with vehemence. "And that makes the girl a mutant! As per UN directive, she must be handed over to the Council for processing and integration. Allocating additional resources and whatever other special treatment that Miss Bagyoko receives will be at our discretion, outside the purview of the administration."

A vein on Rolfe's forehead begins to throb but the Chief Councilman isn't quite done. "And another thing, we're going to be overhauling the Council, put a democratic structure of governance in place. We will now have an elected senate led by a triumvirate."

"Which will undoubtedly be led by you, I'm sure," Rolfe seethes with rage.

"Chief Councilman," the Chief Administrator soothes with an insincere smile. "How you run the Council of Mutant Affairs, I'm sorry, the Senate, and the people is entirely up to you. There are UN guidelines of course..."

"Which have served us well so far," the Chief of the Mutant Council interrupts, "but right now, speaking for the mutated humans of Diablo, we're here to take back one of ours that you have quarantined for observation."

"Fine then," Rolfe says, ducking behind red-tape. "Consider your proposal noted, your request under advisement. We'll need some time to respond. If there's nothing else, I'd like to adjourn this session."

When Rolfe and the Chief Administrator walk into the isolation chamber, they find Kilia undergoing yet another physical. She rises from the examination table soon after and steps up to the glass. "Chief Administrator! I didn't know you'd be coming in to see me today. Anything I can help you with?"

"Kilia," the Chief Administrator begins officiously, "I'd like you to meet the UN Delegate who supervises the workings of our terrarium, among others. He has made the long journey from Geneva to deal with our crisis here."

"Crisis? I'm not sure I understand."

"Good day, Chief Administrator," Khady says breathlessly, as she bursts in through the door. "I got here as soon as I could. Someone from your office called to say you wanted us to meet the UN delegate..."

"Good afternoon, madam," Rolfe extends his hand. "We have something very important we'd like to discuss. Perhaps we should wait till your husband gets here because this concerns you all." Almost as if on cue, Alasco steps into the room and glancing worriedly at his wife's and daughter's faces, asks right away, "Is something wrong with Kilia?"

"No, Mr Bagyoko, not at the moment," the Chief Administrator soothes. "But things may not remain so unless we act now."

"I wasn't the only one to arrive today," Rolfe says, struggling with his impatience. "The newly formed triumvirate of the Diablo Valley graced us with a visit as well. They were here to claim your daughter."

"But Kilia tests negative for radiation poisoning!" Alasco protests, horrified. "And they test her four times a day!"

"Why do the outsiders want her?" Khady questions, her composure surprisingly intact.

"Those foolish outsiders," the Chief Administrator adopts the euphemism gladly, "have this notion that the child might lead to some sort of cure. Pure fantasy, I assure you."

"It's not like the doctors here know what they're dealing with either," Rolfe exclaims, all restraint thrown to the wind. "They're just happy to have something to write and publish their research papers about. Win medals and ribbons."

"And since Kilia's child can't be attributed to anything but mutation," the Chief Administrator plays along, "they're well within their rights."

"What are we going to do?" Khady asks, turning to Alasco.

"The only thing we can," the Chief Administrator soothes, placing his hand on Alasco's shoulder. "We have to stop this sickening science experiment, for your daughter's sake."

"Ar Rashid... Ar Rashid... Ar Rashid..." Alasco repeats feverishly, his eyes clamped shut, crumbling to his knees.

"If we do away with the pregnancy now," the Chief Administrator continues, still soothing, "Kilia will probably make a full recovery. And everything will go back to the way it was."

"But if she doesn't?" Alasco asks, tears brimming in his eyes as he gazes upon his first-born.

"In the worst case," Rolfe replies, "we will have all the genetic material from the unborn child. That should quell any mutation that Kilia might display later on. Either way, there is no downside."

"So, you're telling us that as of now, I'm a mutant?" Kilia, who had so far been a silent witness to the spectacle from the other side of the glass wall, finally speaks. Getting grim nods from both the Chief Administrator and Rolfe, she continues, "Why are you telling us all this now?"

"Because if we don't act now," Rolfe replies, "we won't be able to. Not without putting your life at risk."

Hearing these words, Alasco loses all control over himself. "We should have never come here, Khady," he babbles through tears. "If only we had stayed home... Why did I listen to you..." Feeling just as helpless, Khady hands a kerchief to Alasco and starts rubbing his back.

"We understand the tough position you're in, Mr Bagyoko," Rolfe retires the stick and reaches for the carrot. "I'm at liberty to void the bond you signed when you volunteered with us and offer your entire family free of cost relocation back to Mali should you choose to terminate this pregnancy.

Should you choose to stay here after the procedure, you'd still be entitled to concessions, additional benefits and privileges as well."

The Chief Administrator winces inwardly seeing Rolfe put his cards on the table so early in the game but hoping to make the best of the situation adds, "Unless you wish to condemn your daughter to a life in the Quarantine Zone."

"Concessions?" Khady asks, taken by surprise. "You mean like a bigger apartment? Extra credits?"

The spectacle on the other side of the glass unfolds like a behind-the-scenes segment. A 'making-of' documentary. The actors, bereft of the painstakingly crafted screenplay, flounder about preening in costume and make-up. Each flaw exposed by bad lighting and unflattering camera angles. Their presence diminished by the absence of hyper-realistic setting. Kilia feels the bile well up from within, unsure of what sickens her more—the silver tongues, the naked greed or the all-consuming fear. The words from the oath of citizenship she had taken when she volunteered for the UN mission years ago, which she had repeated with the children she had counselled with Josh on all those graduation days, those very words now reveal themselves for what they really are. Words. On a piece of paper.

"I will not terminate this child," she says with finality, bringing the discussion on the other side to a grinding halt.

"But, Miss Bagyoko," the Chief Administrator says, the first to recover. "You'll be deemed a mutant, be forced to live in the Quarantine Zone forever."

"I understand."

"Then you leave us no choice," Rolfe says, rising abruptly. "You'll be transported to the Quarantine Zone within the hour. You will be housed at the General Hospital for a week.

Should you choose to risk termination at that time, and survive, you are free to return for good. Otherwise, you may visit to bid your family here in the terrarium a final goodbye."

"We'll leave you now to discuss this matter amongst yourselves," the Chief Administrator adds, looking directly at Khady, as he follows Rolfe out.

PRESENT DAY

33

Present Day

Sometimes, the one who got away and the one who never left are one and the same, she muses, one hand on her belly as she reclines on the hospital bed.

Her entrance into the Quarantine Zone had been a bit of an event and the Chief Councilman had come to the walls of the Terrarium to receive her himself. "I could get used to this royal treatment," she had joked. But the official, taking her at face value, remained deferential.

Housed in a refurbished suite and given an all-access pass, she walked through corridors lined with the ailing and the infirm between her regularly scheduled check-ups. Her presence was acknowledged by one and all, with some even asking to be blessed as they knelt before her. The staff referred to her as The Mother.

Staring out of the windows at what she sees of the Quarantine Zone, her thoughts drift to the name she has chosen for her child in memory of the one who slowly and unknowingly warmed her heart.

Just then, there's a knock on the door. After a brief pause Dr Hudson, holding the door ajar asks, "Kilia?"

Hastily wiping the solitary tear making its way down her cheek, she rises to greet him. "Hello, doctor. Do you need more samples, any more tests to be done?"

"No..." The good doctor replies simply, settling down on the only chair in the room.

"It's nice to see you like this," she says, seeing the scientist at ease and without his entourage of doctors and technicians. "I have great news," he begins. "But first, I'd like to know how you're doing. You haven't been feeling stifled, stuck in here these last few days, have you?"

"I'm quite comfortable here, actually," she replies simply, a little puzzled by this tidal shift in Dr Hudson's attitude.

"The Gospel truth, then. Based on the various progressive tests we've made from amniotic fluid samples and the tests we've carried out on those who volunteered, the results are very promising." Catching his breath to check his excitement he continues, "We've determined that it's not just the stem cells your child has been transmitting through the umbilical cord, but its very DNA itself that holds the key to a final solution."

"Really? For all mankind?" Her decision vindicated, a relieved smile spreads across her face.

"Yes," The good doctor replies. "We'll be able to engineer an antidote that we ourselves should be able to manufacture right from here. Hopefully we will be able to formulate a stable inoculation as well. I can't say for sure just yet but in all probability, it will be so. Or as the Pastor prefers to say, *may it be.*

"Now, there is something else I wish to share," the doctor adds, his smile waning just a little. "But you must make a covenant to keep all of it in the strictest confidence."

"Yes, Dr Hudson, of course I do," Kilia replies.

Taking a deep breath, the doctor bares his soul. "Mine has been an influential voice in the resistance, and..." he adds, "I suppose, you know the rest..."

"What?!" she mouths the word inwardly, her lips pursed as she steadies her pulse. The way she has been taught.

"All we wanted was to negotiate," the doctor continues, his

voice laced with fervour. "If we had some sort of leverage, we thought, we could have accomplished something." But sensing the revulsion, Dr Hudson softens his voice. "We only wanted to put the proverbial gun to the head. We never took Josh for such a..."

As Kilia begins to weep with rage, Dr Hudson's voice trails off.

"The child growing in your womb now is more than anything we could have ever hoped for. Ever thought possible." After giving her a moment he adds, "I know these words won't lessen your sorrow, but I truly am sorry."

"It's Josh you should be apologizing to," Kilia replies, now breathing again. "Had he come here instead of getting me back to the terrarium, he would have made it." As she wipes her tears away, she notices Dr Hudson doing the same.

Through his tears the good doctor admits, "When I was left to die a quiet death, he fed me, paid for my weekly antidote, even gave up his allocated housing. He provided." The pain evident on his face, he continues, "And not that it'll matter, but he isn't the only one I lost."

"Why don't you share, doctor? You'll feel better once you do," Kilia responds, her Lacanian training taking over.

"Viktor... he died a dog's death. Put down when he had served his purpose. When he went from asset to liability. It was hard to take then because we hadn't accomplished anything..." Dr Hudson stops mid-sentence."It's only when the invisible hand nudges us forward," he remarks impassively after a moment of contemplation, "that something worthwhile happens. Otherwise it's just bread and circuses all the way."

"I'm sorry, doctor. I don't follow..."

Looking at Kilia, with contentment on his face the doctor explains, "Now we dictate our terms."

THE DAY AFTER

34

Terms & Conditions, Privacy Policy

As Rolfe walks in, followed by the Chief Administrator and No. 2, the Councilmen who had so far been enjoying the view of the Terrarium from the conference room up in the Administrative Office, remain seated. This slight isn't lost on Rolfe but he forces a smile as he takes his seat across the Triumvirate at the oval table.

"Let's get down to business, shall we," the Chief Councilman announces imperiously and begins reading from his iPad.

"In light of the recent developments, we, the people of Diablo, wish to declare our self-sufficiency and outline the terms by which a symbiotic arrangement can continue."

"Now certain that we will be able to develop an effective single-dose antidote from the child's DNA, we no longer require yours any more. We wish to ramp up our hospital, add a wing for research and are willing to negotiate an arrangement to share the products of our studies for untainted human survivors over the world to have a lasting inoculation as well."

"This," David softly interjects, "will eliminate the need to create terrariums as the fallout and contamination spreads."

"Thank you, David," the Chief Councilman says softly, and continues with the terms. "We will provide produce and meat as we have been doing so far, of course, but at revised rates. Whereas, we will trade gold at the same rate the UN gets when dealing with financial markets."

"A price war would hurt us all," David murmurs.

"We wish to commence construction projects in the Quarantine Zone immediately. While we do not feel the need to establish a currency of our own at the moment, the matter is not entirely off the table."

"And finally, we require internet access for all our citizens. Fiber-optic cables will have to be laid and every housing unit will have to be fitted with consoles such as the ones provided to all UN volunteers in here."

"These are our terms. And they are non-negotiable."

"This is what the people want," David adds. "Let's ensure the situation doesn't devolve into chaos..."

Rolfe, his vein throbbing, sits glaring at the Chief Councilman but refuses to comment.

After a long, tense silence, the Chief Administrator speaks, "Perhaps a brief recess is in order."

"*Wunderbar!*" Rolfe says through clenched teeth and marches out immediately, much to the amusement of the Triumvirate.

"David, a word?"

"Look, Davie," the Chief Administrator pleads, his pen clicking in bursts. "We've been developing a mutually beneficial arrangement here, and more importantly, I connect you to the UN, to the world. Are you sure you want to lay out such stiff terms?"

"What has the rest of the world done for us anyway?" David, leaning back in his chair, replies nonchalantly.

"Rest of the world?" the Chief Administrator loses all control over his thumb, "Do you have any idea how you sound? And I thought I was the..." Stopping himself mid-sentence and taking a deep breath, the Chief Administrator starts over. "You may think you're running things, Davie. You're just the poster boy. Those two out there, they'll keep you occupied with cutesy posts on social media the moment internet access is in place. Besides, the child will grow up before you blink... What then? Trust me, I know a five-year plan when I see one. What we offer you, what I offer you, is for life. Besides, the UN will not let this terrarium fail. That would do irreparable damage to us at the negotiating table. Even if it means a dramatic shift in the balance of power amongst nations..."

"As long as the power still rests with the humans, right?" David interrupts. "Save the spiel, Chief." Rising slowly, deliberately from his chair, he leans over the table and gently pries the pen from the Chief Administrator's mortified hand. "I've always fancied this fine writing instrument and think this one's had enough. Why don't you have Paige procure two more? One each for the both of us. I need a new set of equipment to continue my film-making as well. I've already handed over the list to Paige. Do ensure I have it all. And the pen, before Kilia's child is delivered. I'll see you on the next day of rest for some squash," David concludes and strides out as the Chief Administrator, rendered speechless, slumps in his chair in a daze.

Stepping through the turnstiles into the monorail terminal at the base of Tower One with his consorts, he notices Kilia on her way in, on the other side of the track. Excusing himself, he manages to reach her just as she is about to step onto the outbound escalator.

"Miss Bagyoko!" he calls out breathlessly. "Kilia Bagyoko!"

Not recognizing the voice, Kilia steps out of the queue and scans the multitude for a familiar face. "Miss Bagyoko! It's me, David. From the Mutant Council," he says as he catches up to her.

"Councilman David, how may I assist you?"

"You're stealing my lines, Miss," David smiles. "May I offer you a beverage?"

"Thank you, but Dr Hudson and the staff at the hospital have been kind, I'm good."

"I insist! My treat," David presses, gently leading her to the Starbucks nearby.

As they wait for the barista to serve up their order, David starts off. "So how's your family taking all this?"

"They were worried sick but hopefully they'll be able to make their peace, now that we know I'm going to be fine."

"Yes, of course," David replies. "I want you, and them, to know that all of Diablo is with you. Indebted, for the risk you took."

"My parents must be waiting for me," Kilia says between polite sips. "And my brother, he's still underage; my parents wouldn't have been able to tell him much all this while. I can't wait to meet him."

"Right, of course. You probably don't know this but before the apocalypse, I used to make documentaries. I even shot one on the local Sioux community in the reservations around the Diablo region."

"That's nice," Kilia responds, still wondering where the conversation is headed.

"And now I'm preparing for my magnum opus. On your unborn child."

Feeling her throat constrict, she takes a big gulp of the brew. "We'll start shooting the moment you go into labour and follow up at regular intervals, as the child grows, of course," David rambles enthusiastically. "So... have you picked a name for him yet? I have some title ideas that just might help you decide."

As the implications of David's project dawn upon her, Kilia pushes her beverage away.

"I know this may seem like a bit much, but it's a story that needs to be told, Miss Bagyoko. And trust me, you won't even notice us there. I probably shouldn't have told you about this right now, but I wanted you to get comfortable with the idea."

By the time he returns to the chambers of the Mutant Council, he finds Aiko waiting.

Seeing David, she rises abruptly and snarls, "You've summoned me over the non-payment of credits for the apartment, I assume."

"We have much to discuss," he soothes, leading her to one of the smaller offices. "Please..."

"Would you like some water?" he asks once they're seated. When she nods with a little surprise, he pours the drink in one of the glasses there and waits until she has had her fill.

She looks so beautiful when she's angry, he thinks to himself, *even the locks of hair peeping out of her bandages are becoming.* "I know you miss Viktor, Aiko-chan. We all do."

"Miss Viktor?" Aiko asks, stunned by David's familiarity. "Why?"

"Because without him, Aiko-chan, none of this would have been possible. I was in the resistance too." Raising his fist, he softly adds, "For Évolution!"

"You were one of those surgeons?! I knew it. I knew Viktor was killed so that we wouldn't be exposed!" Sitting across wordlessly, David watches on with amusement but is careful not to show it.

"You're yet to tell me why you've called me in but now I have something I want from you," Aiko starts, catching second wind. "Just as we were exonerated by the Triumvirate, I want Viktor's sacrifice to be acknowledged and for him to be honoured."

"In principle, I agree, Aiko-chan. But you have to understand, the situation has changed dramatically. Honestly, I thought about this myself but do we really want the people thinking of all that anymore? And even if we did something in his memory, he would end up a hollow icon, a style statement, at best. Forgotten in essence, reduced to a T-shirt print. Don't get me wrong. Merchandising is good. Merchandising pays the bills, but right now we want to focus on the child. I have played my part, and I assure you. I will persist."

"You? A duplicitous councilman! What have you done?"

"I'm not one to brag, but now that you ask... It was only because of my connection with the Chief Administrator, one that I worked long and hard to forge, that we first learnt of the conception. I then roused both Pastor Felipe and Dr Hudson into action. Both shot and broadcasted their statements. Big risk there, but I managed to throw the scent off. Getting men of science and faith to work together was something even I didn't think possible. Pretty much wrote Dr Hudson's speech. And, I engineered the merger of the Council with the Resistance. I can't take credit for the conception, of course," David adds with a wicked laugh, "but they were my dogged machinations that brought matters to tipping point, both outside the Terrarium, and within."

"Just because you control the information, you think that makes you God?"

"I'm no saviour, Aiko-chan, merely the scribe. And as Viktor died for our cause, I am willing to live for it. That, despite all our outwardly differences, makes us the same. Besides, what I bring to the table has value. It is up to you to judge how much of it I can bring to you. The fact of the matter is, you will be evicted from Viktor's apartment if you don't deposit the dues. Even I can't stop that from happening. And if you have no credits to spare, you'll end up in a tent." After a brief pause he adds, "But if we registered as a couple, we could easily bunk together. I know I'm not your type and I dare not presume. But we could start off as room-mates, see where that takes us."

As the conversation comes together in Aiko's head, a knowing smile appears on her face.

#CliffHanger

"I have just returned from an informal meet with the Chief Councilman," No. 2 reports. "He had come to fetch Kilia and gave me a heads up. The Quarantine Zone-wide referendum for senators will be held within the month. The nominations are already being filed."

Impressed by the pace at which the mutants are moving, the Chief Administrator begins drumming his fingers on the table, his eyes narrowed.

"They have offered us space for a UN office within their proposed settlement," No. 2 continues. "To be staffed, maintained and held fully under our control once it is built. Like an Embassy, you see. But they've requested no such thing from us."

"I suppose we should consider ourselves lucky."

"That's exactly what the Chief Councilman said," No. 2 pipes.

Is the idiot actually gushing? the Chief Administrator wonders, now allowing himself a faint smile of amusement. Misreading derision for approval, No. 2 continues, "Kilia has been handed over." Glancing at the timepiece on the Chief Administrator's desk, he adds, "They should be going through the gates even as we speak."

As the Chief Administrator turns to the display with a nod, Paige toggles through the CCTV network skilfully, finally settling on the camera that tracks Kilia heading out.

At the last check-post, Kilia turns back for one last glance at the world she leaves behind. One hand on her now protruding belly, she stands and waves at the camera.

"Chief, do you think it is Him?" the words escape No. 2's lips as he stares, transfixed, at the poignant visual on the screen.

And he hears his superior reply, "Does it matter?"

● #TheCycleGoesOn　　　　　　　　　　**Follow**　● ● ●

Tammy called today. To say that Pops was finally resting in peace. Not so sure about that, but she sounded chill. Glad she's not bitter any more. Told her what Will told me when he left for the quarantine zone. To follow bliss. *facepalm*

You gotta stop parroting, gurl.

Wonder if Will was following his bliss with Aiko? Or was that his baby all along?

Aarghhh!! #ResetDevice

When the Chief Administrator saw me breakdown, he came back to life. He really is his own Ze & Hir. He got me this, donno what it's called – I'll have to jfgi. But it's a triangle that stands. With a long rectangular base. He put it on my desk on his way out. Got a mug with hot water from the pantry. Asked for one of his green-tea-bags, told me to powder my nose and bring in my clicker.

The thing he put on my desk, all black, has lettering carved on it in gold.

To live in hearts we leave behind is not to die

When I went in and asked what he meant by my clicker, he said with a gentle smile – your iPad, Miss Paige.

It's nearly a quarter to 10. And I'm still here. He keeps dictating, asking for prints, and doing it all over again. I don't know how much longer this will go on, but I'm glad. When he saw me smile as I was explaining how my clicker works, he looked deep into my eyes and said – *Work is worship, is it not?*

Miss you pops.

Be well, Will. You will always exist in my song.

From the Author

Thank you for reading The Carol of the Reactors.
The Trilogy has just begun! If you enjoyed this book,
please consider writing a review on the e-store
of your choice. Your thoughts and opinions
are important to me and will help other readers as well.

www.ingramcontent.com/pod-product-compliance
Lightning Source LLC
LaVergne TN
LVHW042356190726
843493LV00005B/1045